BAKER'S DOZEN

HEY, WAITER!

BAKER'S DOZEN

HEY, WAITER!

Created by Miriam Zakon

Written by Emmy Zitter

MENUCHA PUBLISHERS

Menucha Publishers, Inc.
First published 1993
© 2019 by Menucha Publishers
All rights reserved

ISBN 978-1-61465-684-5
Library of Congress Control Number: 2018942734

Published and distributed by:
Menucha Publishers, Inc.
1235 38th Street
Brooklyn, NY 11218
Tel/Fax: 718-232-0856
www.menuchapublishers.com
sales@menuchapublishers.com

Printed in Israel

Contents

WHO'S WHO IN THE
BAKER'S DOZEN

ASHER BAKER, *age 16. The eldest of the Baker clan, Ashi dorms in a nearby yeshivah — but still manages to take part in the family's adventures!*

BRACHA BAKER, *age 13. It's not easy being the oldest girl in such a large family, especially when you've got five famous sisters just two years younger than you are! But Bracha always rises to the challenge, usually with a smile. Her hobbies are reading, gardening (with her mother), and painting.*

RIVKA BAKER, *age 11. Eldest of the quintuplets, Rivka often tries to mother — and sometimes tries to boss around — her sisters. A talented guitar player with a beautiful voice.*

ZAHAVA BAKER, *age 11. With eleven brothers and sisters, Zahava still manages to get her way. A pretty girl, the kind who gets picked to play Queen Esther in Purim plays, she is usually good-natured, but sometimes high-strung. Her hobbies are drawing, fashion, and needlepoint.*

DINA BAKER, *age 11. Dini is as dependable as her sister Zahava is flighty. She hates injustice and defends the underdog in any fight. Her hobbies include reading and dancing.*

TIKVA BAKER, *age 11. Tikva is blind in one eye and has very poor eyesight in the other; still, she is fiercely independent. Though she cannot see at all in the dark, she refuses to walk with a cane. A very bright girl, she reads all her books in braille. She is shy and reserved with strangers, but at home everyone looks to her for advice and support. Tikva writes poetry in her spare time.*

YOCHEVED BAKER, *age 11. "The Baby Dynamo," as her father calls her, is the smallest of the quints, and a ball of energy and excitement. Yochie's always ready for adventure, quick to anger but quick to forgive. She loves schemes, the more outrageous the better, but rarely thinks about consequences until she's up to her neck in them. Her hobbies change with every new month.*

MOISHY BAKER, *age 9. "He's his father's genius, and my gray hairs," is the way Mrs. Baker describes her difficult prodigy. When he's in the mood, he can memorize hundreds of mishnayos; when he doesn't feel like it, he can fail every math test his teacher gives him. He collects coins and is a computer whiz.*

CHEZKY BAKER, *age 8. A jolly boy, always laughing, terrible in his studies but so good-natured about it that even his teachers have to smile. An expert softball player.*

DONNY BAKER, *age 5. A tough cookie, an independent kid who doesn't care what anyone else thinks of him.*

SARALEH BAKER, *age 3. A sweet little girl, with a dangerous tendency to wandering off.*

RACHEL AHUVA BAKER, *age 1. A fat baby, all cheeks and tummy and legs. She's usually smiling — and why not, with four fathers and seven mothers (besides Abba and Ima)?*

1
Cleaning House

Drip. Plop. Bang. Bang!
  Drip. Plop. Bang. Bang!
  "It's driving me crazy!" groaned Zahava Baker. "Bad enough that we have to be cleaning this place day and night and night and day. But to do it with those workmen always banging in the background and that awful drip, drip, drip all the time! It's like a Chinese water torture!"

"Ah so, so it is!" said Zahava's sister, Yochie, jumping down fearlessly from the stepladder where she'd been standing emptying a closet shelf. Aiming carefully at Zahava, Yochie threw three pairs of dirty socks that had found their way mysteriously to the back corner of the highest shelf, shook a dustball off her nose, crossed her hands in her sleeves, Oriental style, and added in what she hoped was a frightening, sinister voice, "Ve have vays of making you talk!"

"Yochie," groaned her sister Dini. Zahava just rolled her eyes. Tikva laughed out loud.

"Here now, what's going on?" Rivka, the oldest and most organized of the eleven-year-old Baker quints, bustled into the room where the famous sisters were cleaning house, wielding the broomstick that she'd brought upstairs from the kitchen like a dangerous weapon. "Yochie, get back up on that stepladder and quit kidding around all the time! We have lots to do and not much time to do it in. According to my list, we're way behind schedule!"

Yochie stuck her tongue out at Rivka, but she climbed back up on the stepladder and continued searching through the deepest recesses of the closet shelf. For a few moments silence reigned as the quintuplets quietly rummaged through the darkest corners of their room, folded and unfolded clothing, shook out pockets, sorted through old toys and games. Silence reigned — except, of course, for —

Drip. Plop. Bang. Bang! Drip. Plop. Bang. Bang!

Zahava groaned again. "I'm working, I'm working," she muttered to Rivka, who had given her an impatient look. "But I can't help it if that awful drip is driving me buggy!"

Even as she said the word, there was a shriek from Yochie, who jumped down from the stepladder, sailed through the air and landed, miraculously unharmed, on the bed, where the girls had been gathering all the stray pieces of Lego that they'd found. Red, blue, yellow pieces of Lego, little men, miniature trees, and a tiny, wicked-looking cannon went flying into every corner of the room.

"Yochie, what in the...?"

"Are you crazy?"

"Is she okay?"

"Oh, no, look at all that Lego..."

Yochie sat up on the bed with a gasp and a laugh. "Sorry, guys, I didn't mean to do that. But just as Zahava said she was going buggy — I saw one!"

"Saw one what?" four voices asked in unison.

"A buggy! I mean, a bug. There's a monstrous black spider crawling around up there in the closet. It scared me half to death!"

Tikva burst out laughing.

"What's so funny, Tikki?" asked Yochie, indignantly. "Hey, that creepy bug up there almost gave me a heart attack."

Tikva took off her thick glasses, wiped her eyes, and answered, still giggling, "Well, if Zahava said she was going buggy and you ran into a bug, imagine what would have happened if she'd have said she was going batty!"

That did it! The five sisters exploded into laughter, all thought of cleaning and cleaning lists gone. Yochie gathered a handful of Lego that had survived her unexpected landing and threw it merrily around the room. Zahava grabbed some worn-out stuffed animals that had been slated to be given away and flung them back at her sister on the bed. Tikva seized a pillow and threw it. Suddenly the air was full of flying pillows. No more dripping, plopping, or banging now! The only sounds in the room were the girls' puffing and laughing and shouting —

"What in the world is going on here? Yocheved Baker, put down that pillow right now and tell me just what you girls think you are doing!"

Yochie whirled around guiltily, pillow still in hand, to face the wrath of Mrs. Baker.

"Fluffing the bedding?" she answered hesitantly.

Mrs. Baker silenced her with The Look.

"Sorry, Ima, it's my fault," Tikva confessed. "You see, there was this bug, and then we thought, I mean I said, and then there was this bat, I mean..."

"All right, Tikki," Mrs. Baker said, her anger subsiding. She could never stay angry long with any of her girls, but especially not with Tikva, who, legally blind though she was since birth, kept up so gamely with her other sisters. "Look," she continued, "I know it's not much fun around here, what with the leaks from the ceiling and all the other damage from the tornado, not to mention the noise and the dust of the workmen. But Pesach will be here in just a few weeks and we have to get moving with this cleaning — or else!"

"Okay, Ima," a chorus of five chastened voices answered her.

"I'll tell you what, girls," said Mrs. Baker, softening. "Let's leave the bedroom for later, and go to work together in the pantry and kitchen for a while. I was hoping to get something done on the computer today, but I'm just about ready to give up on getting any work done at all at home until after Pesach. That dripping roof and the banging hammers are just driving me crazy!"

"Buggy," said Zahava.

"Batty," said Tikva.

"Nutty, the whole lot of you," said Mrs. Baker, with a grin.

The quints followed their mother happily downstairs to the pantry. They were relieved to be able to leave the bedroom, strewn with its Lego debris, and to go to work with their mother. Even cleaning the pantry would be fun if Ima was there to do it with them!

The girls all still remembered those grim days not long ago when Mrs. Baker had gone to work full-time. It had seemed then to the Baker kids — all twelve of them — that a light had gone out in the old Wharton mansion where the family lived. Fortunately, Mrs. Baker had changed her schedule around, working at her office at Sefer Press only in the morning and trying to get some of her work as a graphics artist done on their computer at home.

This Sunday morning she'd planned to work on the cover of Sefer Press's new cookbook, *Bubby Anna's Best Meals.* But no, she thought ruefully to herself, the cookbook would have to wait; it looked as if she would be doing work in her own kitchen today, along with lots of pairs of hands, ready, willing, and occasionally even able, to help.

The parade of Baker quints raced down the stairs and walked quickly through the massive living room. The five girls stopped for a moment to nod at the electrician working on the light fixture, which had been loosened by the force of the tornado that had struck quiet Bloomfield just a few months ago.

Bloomfield repair crews had been swamped with jobs after the disaster struck, and it seemed to the Bakers that the repairs would go on forever. Sawdust in the dining room, paint chips in the kitchen, the annoying drip, drip, drip of a still leaking roof — the aftermath of that exciting Shabbos tornado, which had found the Baker girls and their friends alone in the cold, dark house — had been delay, dirt, and that endless drip!

As they passed through the dining room, the girls ran into their nine-year-old brother, Moishy, and Chezky, age eight. The two boys were watching interestedly as a gray-haired painter with a walrus mustache scraped off the old, flowered wallpaper on a wall that had cracked.

"What's the hurry, girls?" asked Moishy.

"Terrific surprise in the kitchen!" answered Yochie, with an innocent smile.

"Great! I love surprises!" exclaimed Chezky. The two boys ran off ahead of their sisters.

"Why, Chezky and Moishy! It's nice of you to offer to help clean up also," Mrs. Baker told her boys as they raced in. Before they had time to protest, or to run the other way, she handed them two rags and sent them off to scrub the cabinet under the sink.

"I'll get you for this," Moishy muttered to his sister.

"Nice of you to offer to help," Yochie answered with an angelic look.

Kitchen and pantry were soon abuzz with the sound of cleaning. Scrub that counter! Empty that shelf! Be careful not to miss any corners! Moishy, feeling a bit like a slave himself, began singing *"Avadim Hayinu."* Thirteen-year-old Bracha, the oldest of the Baker girls, joined the crowd, working with Dini on the outside of the refrigerator.

Work was progressing nicely. Mrs. Baker ran from group to group of scrubbing and scraping children, advising here, suggesting there.

Just when Mrs. Baker was beginning to think that maybe, just maybe, they would actually be finished soon and she might get some work done on her cookbook that day after all, in walked five-year-old Donny and three-year-old Saraleh, followed by a toddling Rachel Ahuva. Moishy groaned inwardly. Chezky, less well behaved, groaned outwardly.

"That's not nice!" his sister Rivka admonished him. "They're your brother and sisters."

"They're walking *chametz* factories," retorted Moishy. "Here we are, slaving away on a gorgeous Sunday morning, and they come in to mess everything up! I hate this!"

Mrs. Baker, carrying a cleaning bucket full of soapy water, walked past the children and heard the hushed conversation. She thought for a moment about her own impatience to finish with the Pesach cleaning, and then said quietly, to herself as much as to her children:

"Look, kids, even the little ones want a chance to help. Cleaning our house for Pesach is one mitzvah we can all do together, no matter what the age. What a privilege to prepare our house for Pesach, to turn it into a palace where we can all sit like kings and queens on Seder night!"

She turned to Donny and Saraleh. "Here, you two, come with me. You can help empty out the shelf with all the cans. Let Racheli stack them. I got carried away last week, when tuna fish was on sale. I bet she can make a tuna tower taller than she is!"

Bracha smiled to herself at her mother's words. Good old Ima! She hoped that someday when she was a mother she could also make tough jobs like cleaning for Pesach seem so, well, special.

Bracha's train of thought was rudely interrupted by the ring, ring, ring of the telephone. Hastily, she dropped her rag and ran to pick it up.

"It's Ashi, Ima," she said, her voice thick with curiosity. Sixteen-year-old Ashi, the eldest of the Bakers, rarely called during the week from the nearby yeshivah where he dormed. What could he have to talk about with Ima that couldn't wait until he came home for supper, as he usually did on Wednesday nights?

Mrs. Baker's face was a study as she spoke shortly to her oldest son. "Okay, Ashi. Uh huh. I understand. Abba and I will discuss it later today and get back to you. Yes, all right, before nine o'clock. Bye now."

"What's the matter, Ima? Is everything okay with Ashi?" Bracha asked her mother, concerned.

Mrs. Baker looked at her daughter blankly. "Yes, Bracha, don't worry. Everything's fine."

But as she picked up her cleaning bucket and headed absently out of the kitchen, she didn't sound too certain about that. She didn't seem certain at all.

2
Bracha's Diary #1

Dear Diary,

Big news today! It's about my brother, Ashi. We found out tonight, at dinner, that he's got himself, for the first time ever, a real, live, well-paid job!

Good news, Diary, wouldn't you say? Well, I wouldn't, and neither would any of us Bakers, and I'll tell you why. Ashi is going to be working as a waiter at an elegant hotel up in the mountains. That'd be fine with all of us (when Donny heard the news at the dinner table the first thing he said was, "Great, can he bring us home some fancy desserts?"), except for one little thing. He's going to be working there over Pesach.

Pesach without Ashi! I can hardly imagine it. And let me tell you, Diary, though she won't admit it, I think that Ima is more upset about it than any of us. You should have seen her face when she told us about it at the dinner table. She tried to seem casual, but she looked like she was going to cry.

"Guess what, crowd," she began. "I have some exciting news about Ashi." I was all ears, because Ashi had called up today from yeshivah, which he almost never does during the week, and all day long I'd been wondering and wondering what it was all about.

"Ashi will be getting a job soon, working as a waiter at the Riley Lake Hotel."

Donny made his comment about desserts. Moishy asked curiously how much he'd get paid. Chezky asked eagerly if maybe he could work there, too. And I, unsuspecting, asked — when will he start working?

"He'll be working there — all through Pesach," my mother answered, her voice low.

There was a hushed moment of total, stunned silence, and then — pandemonium!

"You mean that Ashi won't be here for Pesach?" Dini almost shouted.

"Who's going to help me with 'Mah Nishtanah'?" wailed Saraleh.

"Who's going to open the door for Eliyahu?" cried Chezky.

"And who's going to make the cow noises during 'Chad Gadya'?" continued Moishy.

"Waaaaah," added Rachel Ahuva, throwing her mashed potatoes at Tikva for emphasis. When things get loud at the Baker table, she always has to add her share!

Ima and Abba have a pretty high tolerance for noise at mealtimes, but this was getting out of hand. Abba *banged on the table once and then announced: "Now hear this! All Baker kids will sit quietly in their places right now!" That quieted us all down, fast. Even Racheli didn't throw the next handful of potatoes, smearing them neatly into her hair instead.*

"Okay, that's better," Abba continued, sternly. "I know you're all upset about this news, but I want you to understand two things. First off, there is no excuse, none whatsoever, for exploding like that at the table."

We all sat sheepishly as he looked round the table, glaring at each one of us. Tikva discreetly wiped the potatoes off her glasses with a dinner napkin.

"Second of all," continued Abba in a gentler voice, "I want you to know that your mother and I understand how you feel. It's not easy for us, either, thinking about a Pesach Seder without all of us celebrating here together. But this seems to mean a lot to your brother Ashi. He wants to be independent, he wants to earn some money on his own, and we have to respect that." He turned to Ima, as if trying to convince her. "He's growing up. And that's that."

So that, as Abba said, is that. The rest of dinner continued, somewhat quieter than usual. We were all rather subdued by the news. Ima promised that Ashi would be able to come and visit us on his day off during Chol HaMoed, but that was cold comfort. No Ashi this Pesach! Unbelievable!

All evening long, I couldn't forget that we wouldn't see Ashi at the Seder this Pesach. I sat in my room doing my homework, trying to ignore that awful dripping from the roof, and thinking glumly about the next few weeks of Pesach cleaning. This afternoon I had decided to try to look at all the work positively, like Ima had suggested, but it was going to be a lot harder to do now. All that scrubbing and cleaning and checking, and at the end of it all — a Pesach without Ashi.

3
Family Pow-Wows

At the Baker home, a rather quiet few days followed the bombshell about Ashi's upcoming job. Ashi himself came home for supper as usual on Wednesday evening, expecting to receive excited congratulations from the rest of the family. His father shook his hand warmly, man-to-man. His mother gave him a rather wan smile. His brothers and sisters came over, one by one, to wish him *mazal tov*.

"Great news, Ashi," muttered Moishy.

"*Mazal tov*," said Bracha with a dark frown.

"We're thrilled to pieces," added Dini, looking anything but.

"Hey, what's going on?" asked a puzzled Ashi. "I've seen happier faces in a dentist's office waiting room! Aren't you guys happy for me?"

The Baker kids relented.

"Sure, Ashi, we're happy for you," Rivka answered for them all.

"But we will miss you," added Tikva, mournfully.

"I'll miss you guys, too," said Ashi. "But a chance to go off on my own and make some money, and to enjoy myself at a resort hotel in the bargain — it's too good to miss!"

Ashi's enthusiasm was infectious. By the time he returned to yeshivah the next morning, hotel life was topic number one at the Baker home.

"Imagine the desserts he'll get to serve," said five-year-old Donny, who was always hungry.

"Imagine the clothing the women will wear," said Zahava, dreamily. "Do you think Ashi will dress in a tuxedo, with a bow tie?"

"Who cares what he'll wear?" asked Moishy, impatiently. "Imagine the sports he'll get to play. Boating, basketball, swimming, horseback riding..."

"Imagine the shows he'll get to see every night," interrupted Dini.

"Fantastic," said Yochie.

"Double fantastic," said Rivka.

"Triple fantastic, with a cherry on top," said Tikva.

"Which brings us right back to those desserts," sighed Donny.

"Do you think we'll ever get to stay at a resort hotel?" Chezky asked.

"I doubt it," answered Bracha firmly. "Desserts, fashions, pools, sports, shows — those things don't come cheap! Places like that cost a fortune. Which," she added with a sigh, "we certainly don't have around here."

For the next few days, life at the Baker home seemed as far removed from luxury hotel life as *chametz* is from matzah. Nothing luxurious about spending all your free time cleaning and cleaning and cleaning — especially when the house never seems to get any cleaner!

For Pesach this year at the Baker home was an exercise in frustration. Bracha cleaned out the entrance hall, and an hour later three workmen in their heavy boots tracked right through it, leaving a trail of mud behind them. Dini and Rivka polished the wooden moldings in the living room, only to find them covered the next day with a layer of plaster dust after the painter had scraped the ceiling.

The last straw came when two of the workers, who didn't know any better, took their break in the middle of the quints' room and ate their sandwiches at Tikki's desk. The two hungry men sprayed the room, which had finally been cleaned to Mrs. Baker's satisfaction, with crumbs from their Italian bread and sugar cookies. The quints remembered learning about how the Egyptians had tortured their Jewish slaves by undoing every night all that they had built during the day. They knew *exactly* how they felt.

After a few days of intensive Pesach cleaning, Mrs. Baker, despite her intention of remaining cheerful, was at her wits' end. Zlata, the Baker's new housekeeper, had been called to Chicago to nurse an elderly aunt, and she wouldn't return until after Pesach. Household help was impossible to find at this busy time of year, so the family was on its own. Mrs. Baker herself couldn't even begin cleaning the kitchen seriously because the plumber still had to make some repairs around the sink.

So there she was, working at the office in the morning, cleaning the house in the afternoon, recleaning the same places in the evening, after the workers had inevitably messed them up — when was she going to start shopping for Pesach? When was she going to start cooking? Could a household full of sloppy workmen; unhappy, overworked kids; and a tired, harried mother manage to pull Pesach together this year?

It didn't make it any easier that her two strongest workmen, Ashi and Mr. Baker, weren't around to help. Ashi's yeshivah had already closed for *bein hazmanim*, but instead of being around the house as usual, shlepping, scrubbing, and encouraging everybody else with his grin, Ashi had headed straight up to the mountains, where he and his fellow waiters were working hard preparing the hotel for Pesach. Mrs. Baker tried putting a picture of her *bechor* on the kitchen counter to cheer them all up as they cleaned, but it was hardly the same as having him home.

Furthermore, Mr. Baker, who was usually a good though absentminded worker, was also not much of a help this year. He was working late in his backyard office every night, putting together an unusually complex case.

And so it came to be that the Baker family was worn out and grouchy one Tuesday night, two weeks before Pesach, when Mr. Baker announced that there would be a family pow-wow in the den after supper.

"What do you suppose it's about?" asked Bracha, as the kids filed into the room.

"Hey, put away those potato chips," Rivka shrieked at Chezky, who came in crumpling a bag. "Can't you read the sign?" (After the fiasco with the workmen in the quints' room, the Bakers had taken to putting signs on any room that had been cleaned for Pesach. *"No-Chametz Zone — This Means You"* read the sign on the den door, and Chezky had added a picture of a skull and crossbones for dramatic effect.)

"I don't know," said Tikva. "But it had better be good news." She sighed gently. "I'm too tired to think about anything bad."

"Good news? Did I hear somebody asking for good news?" Mr. Baker had bounded in, an enormous smile on his face. "Is everybody here?"

"Anybody who isn't here, please call out your name," intoned Yochie.

"And speak up! People who aren't here have to talk loud to be heard!" added Chezky.

"Sounds to me like there are a number of people here who aren't all there," grumbled Moishy.

Mr. Baker put an end to the conversation. "Here or not here, Baker brood, I've got news — and don't worry, Tikki, it's going to be good!"

"What? What? What is it?" a chorus of voices asked

expectantly. Even Mrs. Baker, who had dragged herself in wearily from her scrubbing, perked up a bit as she awaited her husband's announcement.

"Well, kids, you might have noticed that I haven't been around much these past two weeks. I'm sorry I haven't done my share of cleaning up for Pesach, but I had some important paperwork to finish up for my last patent, the mechanical page-turner for pianists."

Mr. Baker was a patent attorney as well as an inventor, and he was often his own best client. "Anyway, my part in the inventing process is over. I showed the official report about it to somebody at Belmont Pianos, and they liked the concept — and bought the rights!"

"Oh, Abba, how wonderful!" exclaimed Bracha.

"Okay, Abba, how much?" asked Moishy, bluntly.

Mr. Baker gave him a look.

"Enough, young man, to pay for the repairs to the house that weren't covered by insurance and also to pay for a vacation. So what would you people think of spending this coming Pesach — at a resort hotel?"

What would they think? Nobody actually answered that question, because in a moment the den was too noisy for anyone to hear himself think at all. But Mr. Baker didn't have to hear his family's individual comments on his plan to get a sense of the unanimous opinion:

"Pesach in a resort hotel! Fabulous!"

"Most years I wouldn't like the idea that much," Mrs. Baker told her husband. "I like the cooking and baking for Pesach, and I love having the Seder at home. But this year, when it's all been so difficult — it's a miracle!"

"Which hotel will we go to?" asked Bracha.

"I'll make a list of possibilities," said Rivka, reaching for her ever-present pad and pencil.

"How about Grossmans?" suggested Zahava. "I hear they have a fashion show that's unbelievable."

"Hotel on the Hill has a pool where Olympic swimmers practice," said Moishy.

"The Chinns once went to the Mountain Crest and said the food was fantastic," chimed in Dini.

Mrs. Baker spoke up. "Those are all good suggestions," she said. "But actually," she paused and blushed just a little, "actually I was thinking of the Riley Lake Hotel."

"Riley Lake?" repeated Rivka. "Isn't that where...?"

"Where Ashi is working," Mr. Baker completed the sentence and looked hard at his wife.

"Right," said Mrs. Baker, her blush deepening. "The hotel where my Ashi is working."

"Ashi! Ashi! Ashi!" Saraleh hadn't understood all of the conversation, but she knew that she wanted to be with her big brother, wherever that might be. "Ashi! Ashi! Ashi!" she continued chanting.

"Hey, it would be great!" exclaimed Chezky. "We could play all sorts of sports together during Chol HaMoed! Everybody in the pool!"

"And he'd get us doubles on dessert," added Donny enthusiastically.

"Er, dear, I'm a little unsure about this," said Mr. Baker to his wife. "Don't you think that Ashi wants to be, would rather be — independent?"

"Oh, we won't interfere with him at all." The children's enthusiasm made Mrs. Baker feel more sure of the idea herself. "And wouldn't it be wonderful to be under the same roof this Pesach, after all?"

"As long as the roof doesn't leak," quipped Yochie.

"Won't Ashi be happy when we tell him!" said Tikki with a smile.

"Tell him? Why tell him?" said Chezky. "Why not just show up and surprise him! It'll be a great way for him to start his life as a working man!"

The family took up Chezky's suggestion gleefully. Mr. Baker, who still had his doubts about the plan, conceded defeat gracefully and agreed to make the reservations — despite his reservations.

The house still had to be cleaned for Pesach, and the Baker family was busy and working hard for the next two weeks, but with what a difference in their mood. Singing as they scrubbed, joking as they swept, imagining as they mopped — the Baker cleaning staff couldn't be happier! For who could complain about beating mattresses and moving dressers when at the end of it all a week at the Riley Lake Hotel was waiting!

4

Surprise!

"Riley Lake! Smiley Lake! No mistake! No mistake!"

On the road to the Riley Lake Resort Hotel for just over an hour, eleven excited Baker children were chanting, and two tired Baker parents were trying to ignore the noise.

"How did that annoying song get started?" asked Mr. Baker irritably, trying to keep his mind on the crowded road ahead of him.

"A better question would be, how could it be ended?" his wife answered, wincing as Saraleh hit a high note.

"Hey, kids, let's play a game instead," Mr. Baker shouted over the noise, hoping to quiet things down.

"How about Geography?" suggested Moishy. "I'll start. Israel."

"London," said Tikva immediately.

"New York," continued Rivka.

"Kalamazoo," said Chezky.

"No such place," countered Moishy.

"Is too…"

"Is not…"

"Is too…"

"Is not…"

The din was rising again. Mr. Baker honked the horn to get the kids' attention.

"Kalamazoo is a city in Michigan. Go on, letter O."

"Oregon," suggested Mrs. Baker.

"Nebraska," said Dini.

"Australia," shouted Yochie.

"No A's," said Bracha. "You know the Baker Rule: No A's!"

"You mean on your report card, right?" asked Chezky.

"You know what I mean! A's in Geography go on forever, so they're not allowed!"

"Are too…"

"Are not…"

"Are too…"

"Are not…"

Honk! Honk! Mr. Baker got everybody quiet again.

"The no A's rule is a good one, and it holds. Let's start over again. How about Rochester? Any suggestions, gang?"

Even before it started, Mr. Baker knew he'd made the wrong choice.

"Rochester — rrrr. Hmmm…Riley Lake! Right, Riley Lake! Smiley Lake! No mistake! No mistake!"

Mr. Baker groaned. Mrs. Baker opened her pocket-book and took out a small package.

"I bought these for Saraleh, to keep her ears dry when she goes swimming, but I think you need them more."

Happily, Mr. Baker placed the earplugs in his ears and continued driving, listening to the muffled sound of "Riley Lake! Smiley Lake! No mistake! No mistake!" in the background. Just a little while more now — and they would be there! Riley Lake! No mistake!

"No mistakes," said Mr. Heisenpfeffer, head waiter at the Riley Lake Resort Hotel, to his crew of young waiters. "If a guest asks for grapefruit juice, don't bring orange juice. If he asks for a steak well-done, make sure the cook knows about it and does it right. If somebody wants a double portion of soup, don't bring a triple portion of salad." He glared at his waiters from beneath bushy gray eyebrows. "Understood?"

"Yes, Mr. Heisenpfeffer," the boys murmured nervously.

"This hotel has one of the best reputations in the mountains," the head waiter continued, shaking a fist at the crew for emphasis. "It got that reputation because of the attention its staff has always paid to details and to good service." Again, the glare. "Understood?"

"Yes, Mr. Heisenpfeffer," came back the muted answer.

"Up until now you've been working behind the scenes, preparing the rooms and the kitchen. Soon, you

will be going into the dining room. Now, a Riley waiter *looks* like a Riley waiter! Straighten out those bow
ties! Tuck in those shirts! Button those jackets!" The
boys fidgeted a little as Mr. Heinsenpfeffer marched
back and forth, a general inspecting his troops.

"Cohen, that tie is a mess! Rosen, your shoes are
muddy! Baker, comb your hair! Do you want to go into
the dining room looking like a well-used mop?"

"Yes, Mr. Heisenpfeffer. Er, I mean, no, Mr...." Ashi
blushed a deep red. His friend Yudy Friedman, standing next to him, suppressed a grin.

"Okay, men," continued Mr. Heisenpfeffer. "Here
are your table assignments. Cohen, tables one, two and
three. Rosen, four, five, six."

"It's like we're going into battle or something,"
whispered Yudy to Ashi.

"What's that you said, Friedman?" Mr. Heisenpfeffer
growled.

"Nothing, sir," Yudy answered, nervously.

"Pay attention, now! Where was I? Oh, yes, Baker.
Baker, you can have the V.I.P. table. There's some singer and his family going to be sitting there. Could mean
some big tips for you — if you don't mess up." He gave
Ashi a look rather like one he'd give a waiter who had
brought him soup with a bug floating in it. "Think you
can handle it?"

"I'll try my best, sir," answered Ashi, swallowing
hard and trying not to stammer.

"Okay. Most of the waiters have three tables, but
I'll only give you one more. Table 12. Supposed to have

some big family there, lots of kids. They didn't want to sit in the children's dining room."

"Thank you, sir," Ashi answered.

Mr. Heisenpfeffer turned toward Yudy, giving him a rather sly grin. "Speaking of that, Friedman, next comes your assignment. You've got the children's dining room for the next four days."

"Mr. Heisenpfeffer, sir?" Yudy ventured a question. "Why only four days? What happens afterwards?"

But Mr. Heisenpfeffer just glowered at Yudy. "Lunch will be served in half an hour. Be back here in the kitchen in fifteen minutes. You're dismissed." He walked out.

The boys began to disperse, heading toward the wing where the staff had their small rooms.

"Er, Mendy," Yudy ran after one of the more experienced waiters. "What's the story with the children's dining room? Why just four days?"

Menachem Mendel Cohen, who had been coming to Riley Lake for three years now, just shook his head.

"The kids' room? Oh, well, we always rotate that one," he answered in an offhand manner.

"But I don't get it," Yudy persisted. "Why?"

Mendy shook his head. "You'll find out — soon enough," he said. He gave an ironic little smile and added, "Let it be a surprise for you." Then he hurried away.

Ashi and Yudy mused together as they walked towards the tiny cubicle of a room that the hotel had assigned to them, Riley Lake's newest waiters.

"Whew," said Ashi. "Mr. Heisenpfeffer may be a terrific head waiter, but he sure is scary! I feel like a new soldier who just failed inspection because his general discovered that he'd put his boots on the wrong feet."

But Yudy wasn't thinking too much about Mr. Heisenpfeffer, terrifying though the thought of the man was. He was thinking more about what surprise was facing him in just a few minutes in the children's dining room.

"Why do you suppose they rotate it, Ashi? What could go on in there?" he asked his friend.

Ashi ran a hand through his hair, and then, remembering Mr. Heisenpfeffer's comment about the mop, smoothed it down again.

"I don't know, Yudy," he answered. "But you'll find out soon enough."

"Soon enough," echoed his friend in a hollow voice. "Soon enough."

Fifteen minutes later, the boys had no more time for nervous speculation. Lunchtime! All the waiters bustled about the dining room, setting and resetting tables, counting chairs, placing salt and pepper shakers, arranging centerpieces. Everywhere the presence of Mr. Heisenpfeffer loomed, checking, shifting, counting, arranging.

Ashi's tables were very centrally located, not too far from the kitchen. After all, he would be serving the V.I.P.s! He tried his best not to think about that terrifying fact.

At a signal from Mr. Heisenpfeffer, the huge double doors to the dining room were thrown open. The waiters stood by their tables, trying to look dignified. A number of people headed straight for Ashi's V.I.P. table. A middle-aged woman with kindly eyes, a man, probably her husband, a young man with a clipped brown beard who looked a little familiar, a girl about his quint sisters' age — Ashi breathed a small sigh of relief. They might be Very Important People, these V.I.P.s, but they looked like the kind of folks his parents would like. Maybe it wouldn't be that bad, after all!

Ashi took his guests' orders with what he hoped was aplomb. Fortunately, nobody had arrived yet at his other table, so he didn't have to worry about juggling orders. Sweet-smelling, sparkling fresh fruit cups had been set on the table already, along with vegetables and dips — no bread or matzah today, on *erev Pesach*! Now Ashi would have to bring in some soup — onion for the woman, vegetable for everybody else — two orders of fish, assorted cheeses...this was going to be easy!

In the kitchen, all was controlled chaos. Waiters scurried about, holding trays, trying to get the freshest milk and the hottest soup for their guests. Busboys wheeled silverware carts, kitchen aides ran about with peelers, and the main chef hummed to himself as he juggled frying pans and soup ladles.

Ashi took a tray and loaded it up, remembering Mr. Heisenpfeffer's admonitions about balancing it properly. Smoke wafted from the bowls of savory soup.

Better move quickly, Baker, he said to himself, *before it gets cold!*

As fast as he dared, Ashi headed toward the two swinging doors. Remembering Mr. Heisenpfeffer's oft-repeated warning about using the proper doors, he pushed open the exit with his shoulder, executing a neat turn with the tray as he entered the bustling dining room. Out of the corner of one eye he saw Mr. Heisenpfeffer staring in his direction. Out of the corner of the other eye he noted that there seemed to be people sitting now at Table 12, his other table. Looked like a lot of them, too. But there was no time to think about that now. It would take all his concentration to carry the laden tray, which was getting heavier, it seemed, every moment, straight to the V.I.P. table where the woman with the kind eyes and her family were waiting expectantly for their soup. One step at a time, then another, getting closer, easy does it, watch out for chairs, almost there now...

"Surprise!" a thin, high voice piped up out of the heavens. Startled, Ashi whirled around on one foot.

"Hi, Ashi! Surprise!"

Could it be? Impossible! But, no, there they were! Sitting at Table 12, there they were — eleven laughing Baker kids, waving and shouting!

Ashi couldn't believe his eyes. His jaw dropped — and then suddenly, unbelievably, his tray dropped also!

Splat! Four bowls of hot soup started running down the dining room floor. Some of it ricocheted up, hitting the older woman at the V.I.P. table. *Crash!* came the sound of crockery breaking! *Spin!* went Ashi's head and *Boom!* went his heart as he viewed the disaster.

"Surprise!" It was the last word Ashi heard before he had to face one more sound.

"What's all this, Baker?" growled Mr. Heisenpfeffer menacingly. "What's going on here at Table 12?"

5

The Crowd at Table 12

Ashi Baker sat moodily in his room, looking out of the tiny barred window. The best rooms in the hotel were, of course, reserved for the paying guests.

The waiters' rooms overlooked the back of the hotel, and Ashi stared unseeing at the decrepit sheds where the golfing equipment was kept, at the old gardening tractors, at the dumpsters where the trash of two hundred happy, excited, and always hungry guests was dumped. A tawny cat nosed its way delicately around the bright orange dumpsters, looking for stray bits of garbage. *At least I don't have him at my table*, Ashi thought ruefully, getting up from his thin mattress and pacing up and down in the tiny room like some kind of a caged animal.

He thought back wearily to the scene of total bedlam that he'd left just an hour before. "What's all this,

Baker?" Mr. Heisenpfeffer had said to him, furious. "What's going on here at Table 12?"

Ashi remembered with gratitude how his father had taken over amid the awful commotion. Ashi had been too shaken up to think of anything intelligent, or even anything unintelligent, to say to the angry head waiter. Mr. Baker, whose experience as a trial lawyer early in his career had stood him in good stead, rose quickly, introduced himself politely to Mr. Heisenpfeffer, and shook his hand warmly.

"It's my fault, I'm afraid," he said with his most engaging grin. "I'm afraid we rather startled your young waiter here. He thought his family was safely stowed away at home, preparing for Pesach one hundred miles away, and suddenly he sees us sitting at his very own table! You can imagine the shock!"

Mr. Heisenpfeffer could not imagine any shock wild enough to make a waiter of *his* drop a tray, and he still looked none too pleased. But Mr. Baker was a guest, after all, so there was little he could say. He gave him a polite smile, sent Ashi one final, chilling look, and walked back to the kitchen. Mr. Baker got up, too, to go to the registration desk and discuss his family's room assignments.

So Abba had saved him from Mr. Heisenpfeffer's wrath, Ashi thought to himself. But, he added rather bitterly to himself, hadn't he gotten him into this mess in the first place? What in the world were they all doing here?

After Mr. Heisenpfeffer had left, Ashi began to recover from his shock. His first order of business was to apologize profusely to his V.I.P.s.

"I'm so sorry...it was my fault...are you okay...can I help clean you up...unforgivable...please excuse...can I get you more soup...?" the nervous V.I.P. waiter babbled on incoherently, dabbing away helplessly with a lilac-colored dinner napkin at the puddle on the tablecloth.

His guests could not have been more amiable. The older woman gave him a kindly smile. She'd already wiped off the splattered soup from her gray suit (dry-clean only, Ashi noted to himself rather frantically).

"Don't worry about it, young man," she said to him in a soft voice. "Why, I remember the first time my Avi worked in a hotel, many years ago. Not only did he drop a tray of desserts, but he'd gotten all the orders mixed up in the first place! Remember the banana cream pie dropping on the man in his new Yom Tov suit?" she addressed her son with an affectionate smile.

"Do I ever!" the young man with the beard answered with a grin. "The Hotel Horror — unforgettable! I still dream about it at night sometimes, especially after I've eaten banana cream pie."

Ashi suddenly realized why the young man looked so familiar. He'd seen that face before on concert posters and on innumerable cassette labels. Avi? That's right, Avi — Avi Shoham! His V.I.P. was none other than Avi Shoham, the famous singer, and his family. What an honor for Ashi — and what a disaster! Imagine spilling soup on the mother of Avi Shoham, the world renowned singer!

Sitting in his room afterwards thinking about it, Ashi hadn't an inkling of how he had gotten through that meal. The more gracious the Shohams were to their young waiter, the more upset he grew about what he'd done to them at their very first meal, and the more certain he became that something else would go wrong.

And then — and then, there was the small matter of his other table. Table 12.

Gracious? It wasn't exactly the word that Ashi would use to describe the crowd at Table 12. Manic might work better. Possibly bizarre. Or, perhaps more accurately, simply, completely, and totally maddening.

"Hey, Waiter!" Chezky had cried, when Ashi had approached them for their orders. "Hey, Waiter, there's a fly in my soup!"

"What's it doing in there?" Moishy had asked, with a straight face.

"I think it's the backstroke!" The two boys laughed raucously. Ashi looked pained.

Then Yochie asked for juice.

"What kind of juice?" asked her waiter politely.

"*Frum* Jews, of course!" she answered with a giggle.

"Hey, Waiter," cried Moishy. "Hey, Waiter, there's a fly in my soup!"

"Quiet down," replied Chezky, deadpan. "All the other guests will want some, and I gave you the last one!"

"Can I take your order, please?" asked Ashi, with an inward groan.

"Ashi! Ashi! Ashi!" said Saraleh.

"What would you like to eat, Saraleh?" Ashi had turned to his little sister patiently.

"Ashi, bring me a chocolate sandwich with marshmallow cream, peanuts, two scoops of ice cream, and colored sprinkles. Also peanut butter. Please," she added politely.

"Get me the same," said Donny, seriously. "Only make mine with pistachio nuts and chocolate sprinkles. And is there any whipped cream?"

Ashi gave a hollow groan and looked at his mother for help. But she was ignoring the chaos around her, seeing only her oldest son, thinking fondly how handsome he looked in his white shirt and crisp, black bow tie. Her *bechor* — a waiter at an elegant hotel. Imagine!

"Hey, Waiter, there's a fly in my soup!" Moishy began again.

"That'll be ten cents extra, please!" replied his indefatigable brother. The two laughed uproariously, clapped their hands, and upset their water goblets. Rachel Ahuva thought that this was a splendid idea and threw her goblet down, too. Water ran down the edge of the table and made a spreading puddle on the tiled floor.

Suddenly, Ashi heard a peal of laughter from his other table. He whirled around and saw the Shoham family enjoying the spectacle of a virtual flood at the next table. Ashi began thinking about the splitting of the Red Sea and hoping for some kind of miracle to dry the rising waters at the Baker table and to rescue him from this endless lunch.

As if there wasn't enough clamor at Table 12, suddenly five high-pitched voices began shouting, "Idy! Idy! Oh my gosh, it's Idy!" The quints, who had been busy up until now examining the menu voraciously, had just spotted their friend Idy Bodner sitting at the next table.

Idy walked over to see her friends. The quints greeted her warmly. Tikki blushed a little, remembering how they had befriended the new girl in the class when they'd heard that she was related to singer Avi Shoham. Well, good had come out of bad that time, she thought to herself. They hadn't gotten from Idy the free concert tickets that they'd hoped she could provide, but they had gotten to know the shy girl and now counted her among their friends.

"When did you get here?" Rivka asked her excitedly.

"Oh, we just arrived this morning. Isn't this place just too, too gorgeous?"

"We?" asked Dini curiously.

"Yes, my aunt and my uncle and my cousin and me. My parents and the rest of the family will come later in the afternoon. They had some last minute cleaning left to do at home."

"Your cousin? You mean Avi...Avi Shoham is here?" Bracha's eyes opened wide.

"Sure he is. He's right at the table with me. Look over there," Idy answered calmly.

The girls looked. Rivka gasped. Dini caught her breath. Yochie pretended to faint. Avi Shoham himself had his back toward them and didn't see all the excitement that his presence was causing. His cousin Idy looked just a little puzzled. She knew Avi was a terrific singer, but she never could understand the sensation he could cause. It was just her nice Cousin Avi, after all!

The girls chattered excitedly. At the other end of the table, Chezky, Moishy, and Yochie were continuing to drive their waiter to distraction.

"Do you guys want some eggs?" Ashi had asked.

"How about some egg phooey young?" Chezky requested.

"Or eggs Benedict Arnold?" Moishy countered.

"Stop egging him on," interjected Yochie.

At that, Mrs. Baker finally woke up from her reverie, looked at the chaos around her, and began to take control of the table. She ordered scrambled eggs for the boys, eggplant parmesan for the quints, fruit and yogurt for the little ones. She promised Saraleh and Donny that they could pick two desserts from the menu if they ate their whole meal. Remembering the fiasco of the V.I.P. table, she mercifully didn't order soup for anybody. And she asked Ashi to go to the kitchen first and bring back some rags to sop up the puddles of water.

"It feels almost like being at home, doesn't it?" asked Tikva. Her mother just smiled blissfully.

"Yeah," Ashi muttered to himself resentfully as he went into the kitchen to get the cleanup equipment. "Yeah, and that's just what it *shouldn't* feel like. My first job, my first day as waiter — and it's just as crazy as our usual Wednesday night dinner! And what am I going to tell Yudy? Boy, will he ever laugh when he finds out that my family practically followed me over here!"

Ashi didn't have much time to dwell on his troubles, though. As he was loading up his tray in the kitchen with the delicious dishes for his family, Mr. Heisenpfeffer had walked over.

"Baker, I haven't seen such sloppy waiting in all my years here! Dropping the soup on your first day here — unbelievable! You'd better shape up, young man... or else." He paused meaningfully. "Waiters who don't measure up in the main dining room are usually very happy...in the children's room."

Just at that moment the kitchen doors had swung open, and in staggered Yudy Friedman, fresh from the kids' dining room. He was covered with milk stains. A dribble of applesauce ran down his formerly white shirt, racing with a fast-moving line of ketchup. Yudy's face was ashen. Ashi looked at his friend, appalled.

"Remember, Baker, shape up...or else," Mr. Heisenpfeffer repeated grimly, before stalking off.

"How...how is it going in there, Yudy?" Ashi asked his friend in a half-whisper.

But Yudy just shook his head.

"Just three and a half days left. That's ten more meals. I think — I think — I think that *maybe* I'll survive. Maybe." And taking a deep breath he went back into the children's dining room.

Ashi stared after his friend disconsolately. Mr. Heisenpfeffer's words rang in his ears, and continued ringing like a dinner gong gone wild as he finished serving the Shohams and his charges at Table 12, who were just a little calmer now that Mr. Baker had rejoined the table.

He continued to hear the menacing voice as he walked slowly to his tiny room. "Shape up, Baker, or else..."

He thought about those words as he sat by his window and watched the tawny cat finish up his lunch of leftover surprise, neatly lick his paws and whiskers, and curl up under the garbage dumpster to go to sleep peacefully. *Lucky cat*, he thought to himself moodily. He didn't have to face Table 12. Or Mr. Heisenpfeffer!

6
Lobbying

Wow, wasn't that the greatest Seder ever?" crowed Bracha enthusiastically to her sisters.

"The food was certainly terrific. I had no idea that meat that isn't roasted or broiled could taste that good," Rivka added.

"Well, I think that Ima's Seder food is even better," said Chezky loyally.

"We didn't say it wasn't," retorted Rivka. "But wasn't it nice that Ima could sit with us the whole time and that she wasn't too exhausted from cleaning and cooking and serving to enjoy herself also?"

The older Baker kids were sitting in the elegantly decorated lobby of the Riley Lake Resort Hotel, along with many of the other guests who were too awake or too excited or simply too full after the Seder to go to sleep. Mr. and Mrs. Baker had gone up to their room already, carrying a sleeping Rachel Ahuva and Saraleh.

Donny, half asleep, had insisted on staying downstairs with his older brothers and sisters, and he was dozing on Bracha's shoulder as the older ones discussed the night's exciting events.

"The little ones did a fantastic job on '*Mah Nishtanah*,' didn't they?" said Tikva proudly. "And weren't they pleased with their *afikomen* presents!"

"I liked the singing at the end the best," said Moishy. "It was too, too great when the whole Shoham table joined us for '*Echad Mi Yodei'a*'!"

"Too, too loud, maybe," corrected Yochie. But Moishy was feeling good about the Seder — and about singing with Avi Shoham — so he gave up this golden opportunity to get mad or even to answer his sister.

And indeed, it had been a Seder to remember. All the children, even little Rachel Ahuva, had behaved themselves beautifully. Nobody had spilled anything all night long — unless you counted the little bit of wine that had spilled during "*Shefoch Chamascha*," which was obviously the work of none other than Eliyahu HaNavi himself! The songs were wonderful, the *divrei Torah* inspiring, the food and service unbeatable. No, Ashi hadn't made his animal noises at "*Chad Gadya*" — he was too busy and too dignified as a waiter for such games — but the others had made up for it, baaaing and meowing and barking like a veritable farmyard!

"And here's the man whom we owe it all to! The best waiter in the mountains — Ashi Baker himself!" Yochie announced.

The staff at the hotel had held their own Seder, eating quickly so that they could serve the meal during "*Shul-chan Orech*" in the main dining room. Afterwards, they had gathered in the hotel shul to say "*Shir HaShirim*" together. The boys had just finished cleaning and setting up for breakfast, and Ashi was walking along with a group of waiters on their way to their rooms.

As Ashi passed by his family, sitting and chatting in their corner of the lobby, Moishy and Chezky met him with a cheery baaa and meow. "Hey, Waiter!" Dini called merrily to her brother.

Ashi responded to his family's greetings with a distant nod and a cool "*Gut yom tov.*" He was still angry about their behavior at lunch, and resentful that they were here at Riley Lake at all.

"Hey, Baker, what's your hurry? Let's relax right here in the lobby for a little while." Mendy Cohen stopped his friend. "Who can even think about going to sleep after eating a meal like that?" Mendy dropped down heavily into one of the comfortable green and gold armchairs in the Riley Lake lobby.

"Yeah, Ashi, where are you running off to?" Yudy asked his friend with a grin. "Are you that anxious to get back to our five star accommodations?"

"Is it really that bad?" Moishy asked. He and Chezky had made their way shyly to his brother and his friends, sitting at the other side of the lobby.

"Is it really that bad?" echoed Yudy. "No, it's not bad at all if you happen to like banging your head on a low ceiling whenever you try to sit up in your bed."

"Is it really that bad? No, it's not bad at all if you enjoy hearing water dripping in the sink all night long," added Mendy with gusto.

"Is it really that bad? No, it's not bad at all if you love sleeping on a pillow that's been well stuffed with marbles," said Nachum Rosen, another of Ashi's fellow waiters, with a cheerful smile.

"How about you, Ashi?" asked Chezky, hopefully. "How bad would *you* say that your rooms aren't?"

"I would have to say that they're not bad at all," answered Ashi, stiffly. "My room is clean and quite comfortable. I have no complaints to make at all." Chezky's face fell.

An uncomfortable silence followed. Yudy, Mendy, and Nachum got up to leave. Ashi nodded to his brothers and began to follow his friends outside.

The Baker girls had been stunned by Ashi's cold greeting. Had somebody suddenly opened the large picture window in the lobby, that their corner felt so chilly as Ashi walked by? Could this frosty young man in a bow tie be the Ashi who'd made up funny *grammen* about them all on Purim, the Ashi who helped organize their mini-color wars on dull Sundays, the Ashi who had silly nicknames for each and every one of them? Finally, Bracha spoke up.

"Oh, boy. He's mad."

"Double mad," said Yochie, halfheartedly.

"Triple mad," said Chezky gloomily. He and Moishy had trailed back forlornly to where their sisters were sitting after Ashi had walked off with his friends.

"So what do we do now?" asked Rivka.

The Bakers thought hard for a moment. Then Tikva spoke up.

"We have to apologize to him," she said.

"We have to get to him first," pointed out Zahava. "Or get him to come back to us here in the lobby."

Just then, Donny squirmed away from Bracha's shoulder. Idy Bodner, who had been sitting with her friends, looked at the little boy and had an idea.

"Hey, guys, look at what countries do when they want to make peace with each other. They always send a spokesman to help make things up. Why don't you do something similar, and send Donny as your ambassador?"

No sooner said than done! Donny, half asleep though he was, was always happy to go running after older brother Ashi. Donny caught up to him right outside the lobby doors and pleaded with his brother to come back in with him.

"Can't, little guy, I have to go to sleep," Ashi said with a benevolent smile.

"Pleeeeeease, Ashi, I want to show you something important!" Donny pleaded.

"Come on, Baker, go with the kid," said Mendy indulgently.

"Okay, guys, go ahead. I'll catch up in a minute," said Ashi, turning to go back inside with his younger brother. "Now what is it that you want to show me?"

Ashi reentered the lobby, following Donny, who was wide awake now.

"That's what!" cried the five-year-old triumphantly.

"That" was the sight of six Baker girls and two boys sitting on the lobby couch, each waving a white dinner napkin in the classic sign of the vanquished seeking a truce!

Ashi stood motionless for a moment, stunned. Was this crazy family of his just trying to make a fool of him, yet again? Then Bracha spoke up, penitently.

"Er, Ashi," she said, hesitantly.

"Yes?" asked her brother in a voice that could have refrozen the ice cream left over from this afternoon's dessert.

"Uh, Ashi, about today's lunch," Bracha paused for just a moment, and then she burst out. "Oh, Ashi, we're all really sorry about what happened! We didn't mean to startle you so — honestly we didn't! And..." Bracha shot a meaningful glance at Chezky, Moishy, and Yochie, "...and we were pretty mean afterwards, driving you crazy on your first day as waiter. What I want to say is, Ashi, we're really, really, *really* sorry."

"Yeah, Ash, we're sorry," a whole chorus of Baker voices echoed, as the children waved their flags gently.

Ashi tried to remain angry, but his family did look so unhappy — and so funny, with those ridiculous white flags! And it was Pesach, after all — he didn't want his heart to be as hard as Pharaoh's had been, that was for sure!

Ashi stared hard at Chezky, Moishy, and Yochie.

"All right, I'll forgive you — this time. Only there's one condition..."

"What is it?" asked Moishy nervously.

"No more of those blasted flies in that blasted soup!" Ashi burst out laughing. "And you'd better put those dinner napkins back before Mr. Heisenpfeffer sees you with them!"

Relieved, the Baker clan began laughing with him.

"So you really think your room is fine, do you, Ashi?" asked Moishy with a grin.

"Sure it is — it's really fine if you like living in a room that makes Tuki's birdcage look like Pharaoh's palace!"

Once Ashi unbent, the time flew in the late-night lobby. Soon Ashi was entertaining the children with his descriptions of behind-the-scenes kitchen life.

"Let me tell you some of Mendy and Nachum's stories about this place — they've been coming here for years."

And Ashi began to tell them his friends' tales.

"Do you remember that strange bird who was the chef three years ago, Mendy?" Nachum had asked.

"Do I remember? I wish I didn't! He chased me around the kitchen with a meat cleaver after I burned the gravy!" was Mendy's rueful retort.

"Sounds like fun," Yudy interjected. "Almost as much fun as life in the kiddie dining room."

"Still wondering why we rotate that popular job, Baker?" Mendy asked Ashi slyly.

"What goes on in there?" Ashi asked, trying not to seem as anxious as he felt.

Yudy thought about it for a moment, seeking the right words. Then he answered, "Your sisters lived through a tornado, right, Ashi? Well, if you take the energy of that tornado, combine it with the heat of a volcano, the noise of a typhoon, the chaos of a blinding snowstorm...well, you might start getting close."

"Aw, come on, it can't be *that* bad," protested Yochie, interrupting Ashi's stories.

"Exactly what I said to Yudy when he told me that," answered Ashi.

"And what did Yudy say?" asked Zahava, wide-eyed.

"He said, 'It *can* be that bad, and it is.' Like today, he told me what happened at lunchtime. First there was a food fight. All the kids started throwing hard-boiled eggs at each other. Then one of the mothers comes in and asks what's going on, and her seven-year-old son smiles up at her and says, we're making some egg salad!"

Chezky and Moishy hooted. Ashi glared at them.

"It's not funny! Talk about coming out with egg on your face! Then some of the brighter kids decided to booby-trap the kitchen door. They put a big blue cleaning bucket full of soap and lemonade on the top of the door, and when Yudy opened it — kaboom! Enter Yudy Friedman, soapy, soaked, and sticky! And pretty soon it'll be my turn in that house of horrors!" Ashi finished with a shudder.

If Ashi thought that he or Yudy would get some sympathy from his audience, listening raptly, he was very wrong. This time all the Bakers laughed out loud. Ashi continued his lament.

"You should just hear what Yudy says about the kids there. It makes my hair stand on end! There are some older kids who do nothing but make bad jokes and order outrageous foods," he added. The Bakers had the grace to blush, remembering their lunchtime shenanigans.

"What about Mr. Heisenpfeffer? Doesn't he do anything about it?" asked Bracha.

"No, he's pretty much given up on working anything out there," answered Ashi. "As long as the kids are happy, their parents are happy, and as long as the parents are happy, Mr. Heisenpfeffer is...well... you couldn't call him happy about anything, but he's quiet."

"What kind of name is Heisenpfeffer?" asked Idy, curiously.

"Maybe it's Russian for Big Boss or Top Sergeant," suggested Ashi dryly.

"Nah," said his brother, Moishy. "If he's always as angry as you say, Heisenpfeffer must come from Hot Pepper!"

"Why do you suppose Mr. Hot Pepper is always so angry?" asked Yochie.

"Maybe because it's Pesach, so he can't eat any of the waiters before breakfast," answered Chezky, only half kidding.

"I don't know about that," responded Tikva, seriously. "Something really bothers him, that's for sure."

"Yeah, and I know what it is," said Ashi.

"What's that?" they all asked curiously.

"Me," answered Ashi despondently. "And you know that zoo that they call the children's dining room around here? There's not just one kid or a cat or a dog in there — those children are fierce! And if I don't get Mr. Hot Pepper to start liking me, and soon, he's going to stick me in there for good, to be waiter to the lions and tigers and bears."

"And maybe their first course, too," suggested Moishy. The Bakers all sighed.

Poor Ashi!

7
Hotel Life

Hotel life, the Bakers found, was a pleasant enough affair. After their late night in the lobby, they all got a good night's sleep in their comfortable rooms. Even Ashi, in his low-ceilinged, water-dripping, hard-pillowed birdcage, slept the sleep of an honest, and exhausted, workman.

The next morning they all enjoyed davening in the hotel shul, with its warm maroon and gold decor and its stained glass windows depicting the symbols of the twelve *shevatim*. After davening, the girls opted to take a stroll around the lush hotel grounds, in order to work up an appetite for yet another scrumptious hotel meal — one which would not be marred by any flies in the soup, not if they could help it!

The Riley Lake Resort Hotel sprawled over extensive and beautifully maintained grounds. Rolling hills were covered with a thick spread of light green grass, lawns newly awoken from their winter's sleep to celebrate the beginning of spring. Tulips and daffodils bloomed riotously in every color in carefully tended formal flower gardens. Small, dramatic rock gardens dotted the grounds, surrounding surprising centerpieces such as an old well and an antique wooden wine press.

And behind the neatly manicured lawns and gardens, there they stood — the mountains. The air at that altitude was crisp and clear, and it seemed to the city-bred Bakers that they could make out every leaf and pine needle in the dense forests that covered the surrounding mountains. What a beautiful day to go walking on, this — the first day of *Chag HaAviv*!

"Aren't the mountains beautiful?" asked Rivka Baker with a dreamy sigh. "They look so untamed and wild."

"Yeah," said Yochie, never one to admire dramatic vistas, "but no more untamed and wild than the children's dining room that Ashi was telling us about!"

"Do you think it's really that bad?" asked Tikva, concerned.

"Sure sounds like it," answered Bracha, half smiling. "Food fights, mean pranks, spills, messes, tears, tantrums...makes dinner at the Bakers seem like a quiet teatime shared by two elderly ladies!"

"And poor Ashi will have to face it soon, all by himself," sighed Dini.

"Maybe for the rest of Pesach, if Mr. Hot Pepper doesn't start easing up on him," added Yochie grimly.

The girls walked down the well-tended paths in companionable silence. The only sounds were the twittering of birds and the occasional exclamation of wonder and delight at the lovely wildflowers blooming in profusion along the side of the road. Only Dini Baker seemed unaware of the beauty of her surroundings as she walked along slowly, deep in thought, lagging a little behind the others.

Idy Bodner slowed her pace to fall behind with Dini.

"What are you thinking about so hard, Dini?" she asked her friend.

Dini started, half guiltily. "How did you know I was thinking hard?" she asked.

Idy laughed softly. "I noticed that you almost walked off the path into that oak tree, is how! Anybody that can miss a beautiful old oak like that *must* be thinking about something important."

Dini smiled. "Well, it's like this. I've been feeling kind of guilty about getting off so easy this Pesach by coming here to the hotel. We had to clean the house, of course, but we missed all the last minute scrubbing and scraping and shopping and shlepping. All we had to do was pack up our pajamas and our new Pesach dresses, and we were on our way!"

"Hardly reason to complain, I would say," answered Idy comfortably.

"Yeah, I guess not. But still, it feels funny — not really like Pesach at all. And then, there we are, sitting at our table like princesses while Ashi serves us and people we don't even know cook and clean. We don't have to lift a finger to prepare the food or serve it or clear the table or anything. It feels weird to me."

"I know what you mean," agreed Idy. "My mother told me not to bother folding my blankets or making the bed while we're here, because the maid will come in and do it. But that's what hotel living is all about," she finished, rather lamely.

"Well, maybe it is for other people, but I've had just about enough of it already! I want to make myself useful somehow around here."

"But how?" Idy asked her friend, her curiosity aroused. "What could you do? Help Mr. Hot Pepper boss Ashi around in the kitchen?"

The two girls giggled at the thought, and then Dini got serious once again.

"No, but I have another idea," said Dini, mysteriously.

"Tell me!" Idy pleaded with her friend.

The words tumbled out in a rush.

"Well, I've just been thinking that maybe I would offer to help out in the children's dining room! Don't look at me like I'm crazy...everything around here seems to work so well. The cooks cook, the gardeners garden, the waiters wait..."

"The maids maid," added Idy with a laugh.

"Oh, you know what I mean! But the only place that needs help, and I mean *really* needs help, is the children's dining room."

"So what do you think you could do about it, Dini?" asked Idy, her interest piqued.

"Well, I thought that maybe I would volunteer to sit with the kids there and help entertain them and keep order. Sort of like what we all do with Rachel Ahuva when she gets out of hand at mealtime at home! What do you think of it, Idy? Is it a good plan?"

"Well, it's got one major flaw in it, Dini," Idy answered slowly.

"What's that?" Dini looked disappointed.

"That you're planning on trying it — without me!"

"Would you want to do it then, too?" Dini asked her friend eagerly.

"Sure I would, if it's okay with you."

"It's not just okay — it's fabulous! We'll make a terrific team. Let's go find Ashi and discuss it with him right away!"

The two girls said goodbye to the rest of the walkers and turned back quickly to the main building of the hotel. They sought Ashi out in the dining room, where he was carefully laying the table for lunch.

"What's doing, girls?" he asked them, as he efficiently placed each piece of silverware in its exact appointed spot on the dinner napkin.

Excitedly, Dini explained her idea to her brother. Ashi looked dubious. Why would anybody actually *want* to go to the children's dining room, if they didn't absolutely, positively have to? He couldn't understand it in the least. However, he was used to his sisters' harebrained schemes, so he tried to be helpful.

"I guess the thing to do would be to ask permission to try it out," he said calmly, wiping off a half invisible spot on a shining fork.

"Whom do we ask?" the girls cried out together.

Ashi gave them a wicked grin. "I suppose the person to ask would be...Mr. Heisenpfeffer himself."

Dini caught her breath. Go over on their own and speak to the terrifying head waiter?

"Look, girls," Ashi said wisely, sensing their hesitation. "What you want to do will need plenty of courage. I wouldn't try it in a million years! So if you're too scared to face Mr. Hot Pepper, you certainly won't be able to face the terrors of the children's dining room."

Dini looked at her friend. "He's right, you know," she said softly, adding in a firmer voice, "let's go do it!"

Ashi suggested that the two girls look for Mr. Heisenpfeffer in the kitchen or in the hotel's capacious storage rooms. They found him in a back room where the dishes were stored. The head waiter was checking the wine glasses, standing in a row like brave but fragile soldiers, for chips and water spots. Dini was a little surprised that the glasses didn't crack merely from the intensity of his stare. Turning his attention to the two girls, he glared at them from under his bushy gray eyebrows.

"No children in the kitchen area," he roared menacingly.

"Please, sir, we're here to ask you something," said Dini timidly.

"Well, what is it?" the head waiter asked, putting a glass down impatiently.

"Well, we had this idea that maybe we could sit in the children's dining room and help keep order there a little bit. We've heard that the kids can be a bit, well, rowdy now and then, and we hoped we could help out."

"Help out? In the children's dining room?" Mr. Heisenpfeffer waggled his eyebrows disapprovingly, and then, unexpectedly, smiled at the two girls.

"Nice of you two to offer, though I don't know what you little things can do in there. But if you want to try, go ahead. And now," he concluded, gruff and fearsome once again, "didn't I tell you no children in the kitchen area?"

Dini and Idy skipped out happily.

"That wasn't so bad at all, was it?" said Idy.

"No, it wasn't. I'll bet that he's not as mean as the waiters all think. And I'll bet that the kids' room isn't all that terrible, either!"

In that, however, Dini was quite wrong.

8

Lunchtime Lunacy

Mrs. Baker was taken aback by her daughter's offer to help out in the children's dining room.

"But why don't you want to eat with us here?" she asked Dini, unhappy and just a little bit hurt. "Don't you like the food or the service — or the company — in the regular dining room?"

"Look, Ima," explained Dini patiently, "you know that the food, the service, and, most of all, the company in the big dining room can't be beat. But it's just that I feel so, well, so useless, simply sitting around enjoying myself, especially when I know that the waiters in the children's dining room are having such a bad time of it in there."

"I bet that some of the kids are also suffering," added Idy. "It can't be too pleasant for the children who *aren't* making trouble to eat in such a crazy atmosphere."

"And it's not like we wouldn't see the rest of the family during the day, or even eat together for some of the meals," Dini continued, persuasively. "If you'd like, maybe we could eat just one meal together every day — starting with tonight's Seder, of course — and then two in the kids' room. We really think that we can accomplish something worthwhile in there. And Idy's family has agreed already."

"Well..." Mrs. Baker hesitated, torn between her dejection at the thought of the family eating separately and her pride in her daughter for wanting to take on such a daunting task.

"Please, Ima," pleaded Dini, sensing that her mother was wavering.

"What do you think, Ephraim?" Mrs. Baker asked her husband, knowing full well what he would say.

"Well, Shoshana, you realize that you have only yourself to blame if you've gone and raised your daughter to be caring and thoughtful and responsible," answered Mr. Baker, with a smile.

"Ooooh, Abba, then you think we should do it?" squealed Dini, delighted.

"Well, Dini, as long as the two of you are aware of what a tough job you're taking on," answered her father, seriously. "Ashi has told us what goes on in that dining room, and it won't be a simple matter to get it under control."

"Don't worry, Abba, we know all about it," his daughter answered happily. "But we're experts at this sort of thing. We'll have that place running smoothly in less time than it takes you to dip the *karpas* into the salt water!"

"All right, you guys, who put all that salt into the pitcher of water?"

Eight-year-old Leora Gross had just taken a sip of water. A moment later, Leora Gross, coughing and sputtering, had spit the whole thing out right on the table in front of her. Nobody would admit to having poured half the contents of a saltshaker into the ice water, but at the next table seven-year-old twins Moshe and Leib Harris could be seen shaking with laughter.

Lunchtime in the children's dining room was not going very well.

Idy and Dini had thought at first that they would sit separately, lending the weight of their authority to two of the five tables in the children's dining room. When they had walked in as lunch first began, however, the noise had been so, well, so noisy, the hubbub so frightening — the two girls chose instead to sit together to give each other moral support.

And as lunch progressed, Idy and Dini realized that they would need all the support, moral or otherwise, that they could possibly get.

The children were noisy, but controlled, at first, waiting for Kiddush. Saying Kiddush was one of the jobs of the children's waiter. "It's a good thing I get to start the meal with a *brachah*," Yudy Friedman had earlier confided to his friend, Ashi, "because once the meal really gets going, I don't have a prayer!"

Dini and Idy had laughed along with the rest of the Baker family when Ashi had reported his friend's rueful comment. They weren't laughing now.

After Kiddush, there was a mad dash for the sinks for *netilas yadayim.*

"Frontsies backsies!" cried Naomi Steinfeld, pushing ahead of her friend, Miri Freedberg.

"No frontsies backsies!" shouted Ora Heller, pushing Naomi out of the way.

Everyone was pushing and shoving and trying to get in front, until Miri shouted, "Whoever washes first has to be quiet longest!"

"Backsies frontsies!" shouted Naomi Steinfeld, heading for the back of the line.

"No backsies frontsies!" screeched Ora Heller, pushing her backwards toward the front.

Finally, all the children had washed. Most had ignored the clean paper towels set out neatly for their use, choosing instead to wipe their hands on their skirts or pants, or, even more fun, to shake their hands at their fellow lunch eaters and give them a good, cold sprinkling. By the time everybody was sitting, humming and shouting *"Nu"* at each other as they waited for Yudy to say the *brachah* on the matzah, Idy and Dini were appalled — and soaking wet.

And that was just the beginning.

At Table 1, the younger girls' table, mixed drinks were the order of the day. The children ordered orange, apple, tomato, and grape juice from a harassed Yudy, and began mixing them in all sorts of combinations with lemonade and bottles of fizzy cola and orange soda. Two of the girls then added a good dose of salt and pepper, just to keep things interesting.

"Hey, that's *bal tashchis*!" protested Idy. "You can't let all those drinks go to waste!"

"Don't worry," Devorah Schwartz assured her. "They won't go to waste. We'll give it to my little brother Binyamin to drink when we're done. Binny will drink anything!"

But the goings-on at Table 2 made Table 1 seem the model of decorum and table manners. The boys at Table 2 were also interested in different kinds of drinks. Lenny Blumenberg ordered a bottle of seltzer from Yudy.

"Not club soda, not bottled water — real seltzer," he demanded.

"Fussy kid," the unsuspecting Yudy said to himself, as he ran to fill the order. "I thought only grandfathers liked to drink seltzer these days."

And maybe he was right — but if Lenny's grandfather did like to drink seltzer, his eight-year-old grandson enjoyed spritzing the cold, bubbly stuff all over the waiter who brought it so politely to the table!

Dini ran over, trying to reason with the boisterous boys, who were doubled over with laughter as they watched the outraged Yudy drying himself up as best he could with a dinner napkin.

"That was really mean!" she cried, indignantly.

"Hey, a little water never hurt anybody," answered Ronnie Pearl, Lenny's best friend, innocently.

"Yo, Ronnie, did you take a nice shower for Yom Tov?" Lenny called to his friend, aiming his bottle at him and letting the seltzer fly.

"Quit that! Are you crazy or something!" spluttered Ronnie, fuming.

"A little water never hurt anybody," murmured Dini as she returned to her seat, trying to suppress a smile.

But most of the time, smiles were not much in evidence in Dini's and Idy's corner of the table. As lunch progressed, bedlam reigned. Food fights broke out, children shouted and fought and laughed and cried, drinks were spilled, napkins were thrown. Idy and Dini tried reasoning, cajoling, even threatening, but nothing seemed to help. The children's dining room was completely out of control.

"Well, what do we do now?" a discouraged Idy Bodner asked Dini Baker as the two girls walked out of the wreckage of the children's dining room after lunch. Both girls were carrying some fruits and cookies back with them to their rooms. With all the goings-on at lunchtime, neither had found much time or appetite to eat.

"This place looks worse than our house did after the tornado struck," lamented her equally discouraged friend.

"Should we give up, do you think?" asked Idy, afraid to hear the answer.

Dini turned around in the doorway and gazed at the room. Matzah crumbs were everywhere. Puddles of soup and juice lay damply under all the tables. A steak knife stood upright at the center of Table 2, its sharp point stuck tightly into the wood where one of the older boys had thrust it. It quivered ever so gently as a breeze wafted in from the open window nearby, stirring the white curtains, now stained deep purple with grape juice. Bits of broken glass and crockery littered all the tables.

In one corner of the room sat Yudy Friedman, cradling his head in his hands, trying to find the energy to begin cleaning up the devastation of yet another meal in the children's dining room. "Two more days to go, two more days to go," he kept murmuring to himself softly. The two girls stared at the scene, and at the young waiter, awestruck, and then Dini spoke with unexpected firmness.

"Give up? Give up? We Bakers never give up!" Dini looked once more at the shattered dining room and then turned toward her friend with fierce determination. "We'll get this place under control, somehow, Idy," she said staunchly, turning her back on the destruction of the room. "We can do it, Idy. We've just got to."

Lunchtime in the main dining room proceeded in a much more stately fashion. Silverware clinked on fine china, and crystal wine goblets tinkled as waiters carefully poured out bottles of well-aged wine. The gentle hum of conversation was punctuated by more intense voices discussing a point of halachah or a *medrash*, and the mellifluous tones of families singing harmonious *zemiros* together. Even Mr. Heisenpfeffer's astute ears could not discern a discordant note as two hundred content guests enjoyed the delicious lunchtime Yom Tov meal being served in his lovely dining room at the Riley Lake Resort Hotel.

Thus, it was not until he had to serve the soup that Ashi Baker found himself once again — in the soup.

It had started out so well at the V.I.P. table. The table itself looked exquisite; Ashi had spared no pains to make it perfect. The tablecloth was creamy white, edged with real lace. Earlier, Ashi had poured the wine for Kiddush ever-so-carefully into a cut crystal wine bottle, not spilling a drop on the table. The silver of the *becher* and the matching wine *kosos* set out for all the guests gleamed. The lilac napkins picked up and accented the soft pastel color of the silk flower arrangement standing proudly in the center of the table. It was truly a table set for a nation of kings.

Mr. Shoham had said Kiddush with great *kavanah.* His voice was not as powerful or as well trained as his celebrated son's was, but it shared something of the same fervor and sweetness. He said the *brachah* on the matzah with special joy, thinking of all that the *lechem oni* meant to his people, who had emerged from slavery to freedom on this day, generations ago.

The first courses had gone smoothly for Ashi, too. He brought in the elegant fresh fruit cups, followed by the peppery gefilte fish, without incident. Mrs. Shoham had complimented him on the fish as if he had been the one to cook it! The Shoham and Bodner

families talked and laughed, recalling the joys of
the previous night's Seder, remembering stories of
Sedorim in years past. Avi began singing "*Yismechu
BeMalchuscha*," the newest version from his most re-
cent tape, and all the neighboring tables joined in.
Even Ashi had felt relaxed enough for a moment to
stand back and sing a few bars.

Ah, but now it was time to serve the soup.

Remembering the fiasco of yesterday's lunch, Ashi
loaded up his tray with special care, balancing the
steaming bowls and leaving just enough space between
them. He pushed open the doors to the dining room
with his shoulder, turning gracefully with his load toward the V.I.P. table. He was uncomfortably conscious
of Mr. Heisenpfeffer, standing in his usual spot near
the doors, staring at him, it seemed to Ashi, with a
suspicious and unfriendly gleam in his eyes.

No mistakes this time, Ashi thought to himself
grimly, giving Mr. Heisenpfeffer the slightest nod as
he passed his towering figure. Just a few more steps,
now, kiddo, he thought, three, two, one, there, at the
table at last! Ashi sighed with relief as he placed the
tray on the tall stand set up for that purpose. One by
one, his hands steady, Ashi gave out the tomato soup
to his guests, who accepted the bowls and their deli-
cious-smelling contents with thanks.

Done! All the soup had been handed around at the
V.I.P. table. Feeling a new sense of confidence in his
abilities as a waiter, Ashi took his tray and wheeled
around smartly to return to the kitchen. There he

would refill it with bowls of soup for his other table, where the Bakers, much better behaved than yesterday, were sitting waiting patiently for him.

"Uh, Ashi?" Mrs. Shoham's gentle voice followed the young waiter as he began walking away.

"Yes, Mrs. Shoham? Can I get you something else? More matzah? Pickles? Something else to drink? Another bottle of wine?" Ashi asked, anxious to please.

"No, thank you, Ashi," returned Mrs. Shoham with a smile. "Just one thing, please. Could we get some spoons for our soup, do you think?"

Oh, no! Spoons! Desperately, Ashi looked at the table that he'd set with such care and pride. Fish forks and knives — already cleared off. Fruit spoons — gone. Relish fork, meat fork, steak knife, dessert spoons — all still there, shining. But could it possibly be — yes, for all his pains, Ashi had forgotten to set the soup spoons!

Blushing to the roots of his hair, Ashi assured her that he would bring them all their spoons immediately. He hurried off to the kitchen, nodding absently to his family at their table as he passed them by. Mrs. Shoham smiled and turned her attention to the *rav* of the hotel, who had begun saying a *devar Torah* for the whole company.

Spoons — how could he have forgotten the soup spoons! Ashi was furious at himself. He was also puzzled as to what he should do now. As he made his way into the kitchen, Mr. Heisenpfeffer had given him his usual glower. How could he walk past the scowling head waiter now, carrying a dozen soup spoons that should have been set up on the table so much earlier? Mr. Heisenpfeffer would be furious!

I can't just take them in, Ashi thought to himself, desperately. He quietly walked to the corner where the silverware was stored and grabbed the spoons. Thinking quickly, he wrapped them in a large dinner napkin and then stuck the whole package under his suit jacket. *Not an ideal arrangement*, he thought to himself, *but the best I can do under the circumstances.*

All was quiet in the dining room when Ashi tiptoed back in with his secret package. Another brief nod at Mr. Heisenpfeffer. Once again, past the tables where the guests were now listening intently to the words of the *rav* about the four sons of the Haggadah. Such is the wise son, such is the wicked one, such is the simple one...

Crash! It all happened so fast, Ashi never quite figured out how. One moment he was nearing his goal with his contraband spoons carefully secreted under his jacket — and the next moment all twelve spoons had somehow fallen out and landed on the tile floor with a huge clatter!

All eyes in the dining room turned to where the furor had erupted. The *rav* stopped speaking for a moment, and then, eyes full of compassion, continued speaking quickly. The son that didn't know to ask...

Ashi's face was quite as red as the tomato soup. He bent down to pick up the spoons, wiped them quickly with his napkin, and then passed them around at the V.I.P. table. Mrs. Shoham smiled reassuringly at her young waiter. The *rav* finished speaking and the guests turned their full attention to their soup, which was hot and delicious, the incident of the spoons forgotten.

Forgotten, that is, by the guests. But not, most certainly not, forgotten by Mr. Heisenpfeffer. The angry head waiter took Ashi aside after he'd served the roast beef and potatoes.

"Shameful, Baker, simply shameful! Never saw such a thing in my life! I certainly never heard such a commotion in my dining room."

"I'm sorry, sir," answered the contrite Ashi. "It won't happen again."

"It certainly won't, Baker," fumed Mr. Heisenpfeffer. "I'm giving you one more chance, boy. If you don't start acting like a Riley Lake waiter has to act, I'm going to take you away from the V.I.P. table and reassign you permanently — to the children's dining room."

Ashi left the dining room, head bowed, shoulders bent, under a load that seemed much heavier to him than his fully laden soup tray.

9
Ups and Downs

Their first full day at the Riley Lake Resort Hotel passed quickly for the Baker family. Mr. Baker and Ashi enjoyed attending a challenging *Gemara shiur* given after lunch by the hotel *rav*, and then learning together *bechavrusa*.

For Ashi, especially, it was a relief to remove himself from his waiter worries by immersing himself in the complexities of the *Gemara*. Moishy and Chezky went to a class in *Mishnah*, where Moishy wowed the young rebbe by saying twenty-five *mishnayos* by heart. He knew at least twenty-five more, but he was too modest to say so!

Mrs. Baker had been asked by the *rav* to prepare a class for the older girls. The quints, Bracha, Idy, and several other girls from the hotel sat with her under the spreading branches of a flowering chestnut tree, spiritedly discussing the story of *yetzias Mitzrayim* and preparing *divrei Torah* for the second Seder. Afterwards, the girls went for another short stroll before heading for their rooms for a nap. After all, that night they'd be up late again, reveling in yet another beautiful Riley Lake Seder!

They ambled past the mini-golf course, admiring the tiny windmill, the miniature farmhouse, the exquisite castle with its battlements, drawbridge, and cheerful flag.

"I wish Yom Tov would never end. It's so peaceful, just walking and talking and learning..." Bracha said meditatively.

"And eating," inserted Yochie.

"That, certainly," agreed Bracha.

"Peaceful? That's not exactly what I'd call our time at lunch today," said Idy, only half smiling.

"Was it really awful?" asked Zahava.

"Well, it was kind of discouraging," answered Dini with a sigh. "We thought that we'd have everything under control in no time at all. Now, after just one meal in that kids' dining room, I'm beginning to think it'll take a lot longer..."

"Like maybe until Shavuos," Idy put in.

"Of next year," added Dini.

"Well, I think you girls are really brave to try it, and I'm sure you'll figure out how to get things more settled," said Tikva, encouragingly.

"Yeah, like maybe tying all of the children to their chairs and gagging them would do the trick!" suggested Yochie, always helpful.

The girls walked on quietly for a few more minutes, and then Bracha went on with her thought.

"Still, even with your dining room problems, don't
you wish Yom Tov would go on for a few more days?"

"Well, it's been lovely so far, but I'm also looking
forward to Chol HaMoed, when we can go swimming
and boating and stuff," answered Rivka.

"Yeah, and then there's also the concert..." Idy never had a chance to finish her sentence, because six delighted Bakers jumped on her words.

"Concert? What concert? Who? When? Where?"
The usually quiet forest pathways around Riley Lake
rang with their noisy excitement.

"Oh, didn't you know?" asked Idy. "On *motza'ei
Yom Tov*, my cousin Avi is going to perform in concert."

"Where?" asked Rivka, her eyes shining.

"Right here, at Riley Lake! It'll be open to people
from other hotels and bungalows in the area, and Avi
says that they expect a huge turnout, but Riley Lake
guests will be seated in a special section, right up
front!"

"An Avi Shoham concert! A special section! Ooooh
— it's delicious!" gushed Zahava.

"You know, we heard him singing last night at the
Seder, and you'd think that would make it less exciting, but really, the more I hear him the more I want to
hear," said Bracha.

"What do you think he'll sing?" Zahava asked Idy
curiously.

"Well, I know he likes to try to balance his program, performing some of his popular songs and introducing some new ones. And he'll certainly sing some Pesach songs — maybe even some that he sang at the Seder!" Idy answered happily.

Soon afterwards, the girls turned their steps back toward the hotel, where they'd promised Mrs. Baker to return in time for a good, long afternoon rest. The seven girls entered the hotel lobby, their faces a little flushed both with the exertion of their uphill walk home and with the excitement of Idy's bombshell. Yes, perhaps Yom Tov would come to an end too quickly — but it would be followed by a special Chol HaMoed concert by world-famous singer Avi Shoham, right here at Riley Lake!

The second Seder that night at the hotel was as good, or maybe even better, than the first. Once again, the Baker family enjoyed telling and retelling the story of *yetzias Mitzrayim*, saying *divrei Torah* about the Haggadah, singing the well-known songs of Pesach. Once again, the Baker family joined the Shohams and Bodners for the final joyous songs, and they all especially relished singing "*Echad Mi Yodei'a*" and "*Chad Gadya*" with Avi Shoham, knowing that he might sing the very same songs at his concert tomorrow night. What better *afikomen* present, thought the older children to themselves, than to have a pre-concert concert with Avi Shoham!

The only Baker who didn't enjoy himself totally that night was Ashi. Not that there was anything lacking at his Seder. On the contrary, the staff Seder, led by the *rav* of the hotel, was uplifting, and the waiters were as lively as anybody could want. And nothing actually went wrong for Ashi as he served his two tables. He didn't mix up any orders, he didn't spill anything, he didn't forget anything. He even remembered to put the salt in the water for the *karpas* and to fill Eliyahu's beautiful silver goblet before "*Shefoch Chamascha.*"

Nevertheless, throughout the evening, Ashi could never relax. He always had the feeling that Mr. Heisenpfeffer was watching him dourly. Every move he made seemed fraught with peril; every tray he carried seemed loaded with disaster. The head waiter's angry words echoed through his head: "If you don't start acting like a Riley Lake waiter has to act, I'm going to take you away from the V.I.P. table and reassign you permanently — to the children's dining room."

It wouldn't be quite as bad as suffering the ten plagues, Ashi thought grimly to himself, but it still would be an awful fate. It wasn't so much the fact that he would have to face the horrors of the children's dining room for the rest of Pesach, though that certainly was grave enough. No, it was the idea that he might fail — fail his family, fail his guests, and most of all, fail himself, at his very first job — that made Ashi carry each tray as if it were laden with the most delicate and fragile crystal, or the most volatile and dangerous gunpowder.

Ashi's tension did not escape his parents' concerned eyes. At one point during the meal, Mr. Baker turned to his wife and said to her softly, "You know,

Shoshana, how you always say we must go through a 'Baker's dozen' dozen eggs on *erev Pesach*? Well, it looks to me like our son is walking on all the eggshells that the hotel cook cracked open for the Seder."

Mrs. Baker smiled a little, but her eyes looked worried.

Ashi continued his eggshell-walking act the entire second day of Yom Tov. Once again, nothing actually went wrong, but in his imagination everything that could — did. Mr. Heisenpfeffer seemed to Ashi to be watching his every move, a tiger about to pounce.

Once, there was a crash in the dining room, as one of the guests at Mendy's table knocked over a bottle of grape juice. To Ashi's fevered imagination, it seemed that Mr. Heisenpfeffer looked immediately in his direction, certain that Baker had finally made his last mistake in the main dining room.

And if eggshells were the order of the day for Ashi Baker, they also played a large part in the scene in the children's dining room. The second day of Yom Tov there was no more orderly than the first. Yudy had banned seltzer from the kids' dining room for the rest of Pesach, but at breakfast four of the boys at Lenny Blumenberg's table had ordered soft-boiled eggs, and they promptly began an egg spinning contest to see who could get his egg to reach the end of the table first. Eggs, however, are very poor judges of finish lines, and three out of four of them ended up spinning to the floor with a crash and a splat. Poor Yudy had to walk on eggshells much more literally than his friend Ashi did!

Idy and Dini did their best, but with no more success than on the previous day. By the time Yudy came around with the dessert cart, the two girls were hoarse with shouting at the children and exhausted with their efforts to calm them down.

They didn't watch, therefore, as their young charges charged the dessert cart. Naomi Steinfeld and Ora Heller reached the cart at the same time. They both headed straight for the lemon meringue pie lying lusciously on the top shelf. Naomi grabbed it from the right side, Ora from the left; Naomi pulled to the right, Ora pulled to the left; Naomi pulled harder; Ora pulled even harder; until, suddenly, both girls fell over, and the pie went flying — right onto little Binny Schwartz's unsuspecting head!

"Hey, you can't do that to my little brother," shouted big sister Devorah Schwartz, grabbing a piece of seven-layer cake and throwing it at Naomi.

"Hey, you can't do that to my friend," shouted Miri Freedberg, grabbing a hunk of chocolate mousse pie and flinging it at Devorah. Unfortunately, she hit Ronnie Pearl instead, and suddenly all the children were at the dessert cart, grabbing cookies and cakes and pieces of pie and throwing them at each other. Idy got socked by a flying macaroon. Dini got hit by a piece of mandelbroidt sailing gracefully by. Only little Binny Schwartz stayed out of the fray, sitting quietly under the table and blissfully licking off the whipped cream from his hands and face.

Yudy restored order by grabbing the dessert cart and running with it for his life. When the free-for-all ended, Idy and Dini staggered out, not even bothering this time to look behind them at the wreckage.

"Still game to keep trying?" Idy asked her friend weakly.

"We'll do it yet, Idy," said Dini, with more confidence than she felt. Straightening her shoulders as she left the room, Dini brushed off crumbs of mandelbroidt from her dress, and they fell and scattered onto the littered floor.

The Bakers passed the remainder of the second day of Yom Tov in much the same manner as the first. Learning, walking, talking — the time went by pleasantly and quickly. Lunchtime found the children in the kids' dining room a bit more subdued. Enough of the parents had been upset by the sight of chocolate mousse on new white shirts and lemon meringue in freshly washed hair to give their children a strong talking-to. Lenny Blumenberg was notably absent from the boys' table, as was Ronnie Pearl. Both boys were eating with their families at lunch. (In fact, it was Ronnie who spilled the grape juice that so alarmed Ashi!)

Nonetheless, there was still plenty of pushing and jostling to be the first or the last for washing, lots of food was thrown around or spilled, and Idy and Dini still came out of the dining room after lunch feeling that a meal spent in a cage with three lions who'd been fasting for a week might have been more restful.

It was with some relief, then, that the two girls joined the rest of the family in the main dining room for a light supper before Havdalah.

After Havdalah, the family raced to their rooms to begin the long process of deciding what to wear to the concert. Skirt and blouse and sweater? Another Shabbos dress? Hair up? Hair down? Black shoes? Pocketbooks?

The Baker girls ran from room to room, asking, advising, borrowing, swapping, and generally enjoying a frenzy of preparation for the all-important concert. Even Chezky and Moishy, though they mocked their sisters and laughed at their preparations, managed to brush their hair and to change shirts, and Moishy spent a full five minutes trying to decide which tie to wear. Special sections in special concerts call for special measures!

Ashi, of course, couldn't run back to his room after Havdalah. He had to stay and clear the tables, help clean the dining room, and set up for tomorrow's breakfast. Just as he finished laying the silverware (remember the spoons this time, Baker!) on the V.I.P. table, Ashi was surprised to see Mrs. Shoham approaching him.

"A *gutten moed*, Ashi," Mrs. Shoham began pleasantly. "I wonder if I can ask you for something special?"

"Sure, whatever you'd like," Ashi answered quickly.

"Well, I'm sorry to ask you this so late, but I didn't want to talk about it on Yom Tov, and I couldn't speak right after Havdalah because Avi would have heard. You see, it's his birthday on Chol HaMoed. He'll be leaving back to the city tomorrow morning right after breakfast to prepare for his big Chol HaMoed concert, so I thought it would be nice to surprise him with a birthday cake at breakfast."

"What a nice idea, Mrs. Shoham!"

Mrs. Shoham smiled. "I'm glad you think so, Ashi. I hope there will be enough time to prepare it."

"No problem, Mrs. Shoham," Ashi said confidently. "I'm sure the cook will be glad to whip up something nice."

"That's all settled, then. Avi will be so pleased," said Mrs. Shoham, turning around to go. Then she turned back to Ashi and gave him a grateful smile. "You know, Ashi, you've been doing a wonderful job serving our table." Ashi blushed, thinking that Mr. Heisenpfeffer would scarcely agree. "You make us feel like honored guests. We really appreciate that." She walked out of the dining room with a final smile.

Ashi was charmed. He finished setting the table quickly, and then left to go to the kitchen to tell the cook about the cake, pleased to be able to do something for the family that had treated him with such kindness, despite his mistakes.

On the way to the kitchen, though, Ashi heard the clang-clang-clang of an alarm. He hastened out to the lobby to see where it was coming from. The guests were milling around, unsure of what to do.

"Is it a fire alarm?" an elderly man asked nervously.

"No, no," the desk clerk assured him. "It's just the elevator alarm."

"Somebody's stuck in the elevator! Get help!" The shout went round the frightened guests.

Ashi ran off, bounding up the steps two at a time to get to the roof of the building, where the manual controls to the elevator could be found. His imagination also moved in leaps and bounds, as he envisioned elderly guests having heart attacks out of fear or children panicking, trapped in the dark elevator.

Just as he reached the fourth floor, with two more floors to go, he was surprised to see the elevator stopping by itself. Catching his breath, he ran to the door. It opened suddenly, and out stepped — Donny and Saraleh Baker!

"What are you guys doing here?" Ashi asked, when the initial shock had subsided.

It took some doing to get the story out of them, but Ashi finally figured it out. With all their big brothers and sisters busy getting ready for the concert, the two younger Bakers had been bored. They decided to kill time by riding up and down in the service elevator. Going down was simple; but once they were down in the basement, Donny found he couldn't reach the fourth floor button to get back to his room again! With Baker ingenuity, Donny had his little sister climb up on his shoulders to press the button. "Just hit the one that says four," he said, and she promptly went and put her finger on the alarm!

It took Ashi a few moments to return his brother and sister to their parents and to race back downstairs to assure the guests that all was now well. By the time all the explanations were made, it was almost time for the concert. Ashi hurried to his room to change his clothing, and then dashed back to the kitchen to help prepare some light refreshments for intermission. In the lobby, people from Riley Lake and from all the nearby resorts were streaming in for the concert — there was no time to waste if he was to be in time for the opening numbers!

Finally, all was ready. At a curt nod from Mr. Heisenpfeffer, Ashi and the other waiters tore out of the kitchen and headed for the concert. The lights had just dimmed, and the emcee was introducing the star of the evening: "Ladies and Gentlemen, Mr. Avi Shoham!"

Ashi sat in the back row with the other waiters. Something nagged at him in the back of his mind. What was it? Something he'd forgotten? Something he had to do?

On stage, Avi Shoham was beginning a medley of Pesach melodies. The audience clapped along enthusiastically. Lights flashed, and the orchestra played in ringing tones. Ashi began to relax for the first time in days. This would be one great concert. Whatever it was that he'd forgotten could wait. It couldn't be too important — certainly couldn't be as important as a concert starring Avi Shoham himself. "*Echad mi yodei'a?*" sang Avi, using the same tune as he had last night. "*Echad ani yodei'a*," hummed Ashi to himself. Ashi sat back in his seat contentedly, comfortably lost in the music surrounding him.

10
Birthday Blues

Wasn't that too, too dreamy?"

"I'd say, it was more, well, entertaining, than dreamy."

"You're both wrong! It was too real to be dreamy, too inspiring to be just entertaining..."

"So what would you say it was? How would you describe the concert?"

"I'd say it was...awesome!"

Though they differed on what words to use to describe the concert, all the Bakers agreed that it had been a night to remember. Moishy and Chezky and Ashi were still backstage, where they hoped to get Avi to autograph their concert programs. The girls were standing about excitedly in a corner of the Riley Lake lobby, happily chattering about the musical evening.

Avi Shoham had surpassed himself tonight. Not only had he sung beautifully, he had gotten the audience to sing along, and he had even invited some of the guests onstage to join him in duets and trios. The audience had clapped along to the old Pesach tunes, had thrilled to the exciting beat of the newer songs, had cried a little at a sad Yiddish ballad that Avi himself had written, had exulted in the final strains of "*Le-Shanah HaBa'ah BeYerushalayim.*" Dreamy, inspiring, entertaining...awesome!

The best part of the concert, though, came at the end. All the ladies were invited to go out on the luxurious terrace next to the large auditorium. There, under the cold, twinkling stars glinting in the clear air like diamonds, the girls had danced to the strains of the orchestra. Skirts twirling, heads whirling, feet flying, the Baker girls had joined the huge circle of dancing women, their brightly colored dresses making a living, spinning rainbow of color against the black mountain sky. Gorgeous!

After the dancing, the whole audience had gone back inside to cool down from the dance, to warm up from the cold, and to get some refreshments. The Baker girls, Idy Bodner, and several of their new hotel friends had loaded up their plates with fresh fruits, luscious cakes, and delicious raspberry ice cream, and had headed for their corner of the lobby. Once they agreed on "awesome" as the word for the concert, the girls were able to settle down to some serious eating, punctuated by frequent exclamations about the wonder of the night.

Just as Tikva was recounting, for the twelfth time at least, the story that Avi had told on stage about how he'd come to write a Yiddish song, Ashi, Moishy and Chezky burst into the lobby.

"Check this out! Look what we got!" the two younger boys exclaimed, bursting with their news. Ashi followed them, quiet but beaming and clearly as excited as his brothers.

"What is it? What is it?" The Baker girls crowded around their brothers expectantly.

"What is it? It's Avi Shoham's newest CD, that's what it is! And it's autographed, to boot!"

The girls ooohed and aaaahed at the boys' gift. "Avi Shoham's Greatest Hits" had not been released yet to the general public. The Baker family had even beat Borenstein's, Bloomfield's *seforim* and music shop, to the punch. What a triumph!

"Isn't it something?" asked Zahava, gently touching the album cover, with its picture of Avi on stage.

"Isn't *he* something?" asked Ashi seriously, really impressed with the young singer's talent and his consideration.

The talk about the concert went on for a few more minutes. Mr. and Mrs. Baker had gone upstairs immediately after the concert, to put Donny and Saraleh to sleep. A little while later, Mr. Baker came back down to the lobby, holding Rachel Ahuva in his hands. The feisty littlest Baker had stayed up until the end of the concert, and still had enough energy to insist on coming down to help her Abba gather the rest of his family.

"Abba, Abba, look what Avi Shoham gave us!" Moishy shouted when he saw his father.

Mr. Baker smiled broadly at his children's excitement. He, too, was impressed with the generous gift.

"That was really nice of him," he told his children sincerely. Then he looked at his watch. "But do you kids realize that it's past midnight already? Anybody around here ready for bed?"

"Actually, I am," said Bracha, getting up a bit wearily from the comfortable lobby couch. "I feel like I haven't slept for days."

The others agreed with Bracha. They had had many late nights this week, and the vigorous dancing after the concert had tired them all out.

Saying goodnight to their friends, the Bakers gathered up their plates, piled them on the tray set out for that purpose, and headed back to their rooms. Ashi walked them toward the elevator.

"You sure you can all reach the button for the fourth floor?" he asked with a grin, remembering the exciting elevator episode earlier that night.

"We can always ask Rachel Ahuva to press the alarm for us," answered Moishy, with an answering grin.

"Forget it! She's fast asleep already!" Rivka pointed out. And, indeed, the tired baby had cuddled herself up cozily on Mr. Baker's shoulder, thumb in mouth, and was sleeping soundly.

"Boy, isn't she the cutest thing when she's asleep?" cooed Dini.

"How old is she?" asked Idy, smiling gently at the sleeping child.

"She's just about a year old," answered Mr. Baker proudly. "Do you believe that a whole year has gone by since she was born?"

"Hey, that's right," said Chezky. "Her birthday is the week after Pesach, isn't it?"

"It sure is," answered Mr. Baker, softly shifting the baby to his other shoulder. "That gives us plenty of time to start planning her party. Soon after Pesach, we'll have to bake her a spectacular birthday cake — her very first one!" With that, Mr. Baker got into the elevator with Chezky and Moishy. "The rest of you guys come up in the next load, okay?"

The elevator doors shut with a bang. The hotel suddenly seemed very silent — except for the sound of Ashi catching his breath quickly. Birthday? Birthday! Birthday cake!

The Baker girls turned to look at their brother, whose face suddenly looked whiter than a sheet — or than the chef's famous whipped cream frosting. Birthday cake!

"Ashi! What's wrong? What's the matter? What happened?" they cried out together.

"Birthday cake! Oh no, I don't believe it! I forgot all about the birthday cake!"

It didn't take long for Ashi to tell his sisters what had happened. In all the confusion of the clanging elevator and the hustle and bustle surrounding the concert, he had completely forgotten to order the cake for Avi Shoham's special birthday breakfast!

"But what's the problem, Ashi? Can't you just go ask the chef to bake it now?" asked Yochie, always the optimist.

"No, of course not. The kitchen is locked. The chef went to sleep long ago."

"Are you sure?"

"Yeah, I'm sure. Mr. Heisenpfeffer specifically told us waiters that we should put the trays loaded with the dirty dishes right outside the kitchen door, and he'd get them inside and put them in the dishwasher early tomorrow morning." At the mention of Mr. Hot Pepper, Ashi gave a tormented groan. What would the head waiter say if he found out about this latest goof? Maybe he wasn't even fit to serve in the children's dining room!

"Maybe you can explain to Mrs. Shoham what happened and serve the cake at lunch. That'll give the chef plenty of time to bake it," suggested Tikva hopefully.

"No. Avi's leaving the hotel right after breakfast," Ashi answered his sister miserably.

There was a leaden silence for a few moments. Then Bracha spoke up, gently.

"Cheer up, Ashi. It's not the end of the world. It's just a silly birthday cake, after all."

"Yeah, Ash," added Rivka. "And Mrs. Shoham is so nice. I'm sure she'll understand."

"But that's just it," Ashi answered his sisters disconsolately. "It's not just getting into trouble with Mr. Heisenpfeffer. It's much more than that. It's letting

Mrs. Shoham — and Avi — down..." *And myself, too*, he thought to himself bitterly. *Myself, most of all.*

Yochie interrupted him. "We could ask Ima..."

"No!" Ashi said the word explosively. "I don't want Ima or Abba to help. This was supposed to be my job, my first real job.."

"You tried your best, Ashi," said Tikva softly.

"I tried — and I failed! Look, it's nice of you girls to try to cheer me up, but you can't get away from it. I'm a failure as a waiter. I was careless, and I messed up, and there's nothing that you or I or anybody else can do now."

Ashi's pronouncement had a note of finality in it. It was followed by a gloomy silence. His last words lingered in the air, a grim echo of the happy sounds of the evening, the music, the laughter, the excited talk, all forgotten now. "I'm a failure as a waiter. I was careless, and I messed up, and there's nothing that you or I or anybody else can do now."

"Nothing that you can do? Nothing that we can do? Ashi, you're wrong! There's something that you can do!" Yochie's voice, shrill with excitement, broke the spell of gloom that had descended on the Bakers. "Of course there's something that we can do. Let's get back to our corner of the lobby — I've got an idea!"

11
Yochie's Plan

"Okay, Yochie, out with it. What's the plan?" The Baker kids were seated in their corner of the lobby once again. Most of the guests had already left, weary from the day's excitement and the night's entertainment. One old man sat dozing in an armchair, snoring gently, a newspaper folded neatly in his lap. A young man sat quietly, reading a *sefer* intently. Two older boys concentrated on a game of chess.

The Bakers spoke softly, not wanting to disturb the peace and repose of the other guests, but the tumult of their emotions filled the air in their corner with a restless excitement. First there had been their deep despondency at Ashi's predicament, and now there was a sudden surge of hope at Yochie's words. What was her plan?

"It's simple," Yochie said. "Avi Shoham needs a cake for breakfast tomorrow. Ashi has to get it for him. All we have to do is get some sort of cake!"

"That's it?" asked Ashi, crestfallen. "Gee, Yochie, I thought you had something helpful to tell us."

"Wait a minute," said Tikva, speaking slowly, thinking and imagining and planning as she spoke. "Maybe Yochie's idea isn't a bad one, at all."

"But Tikva," protested Ashi, "where in the world are we going to get a cake? We're here in the middle of nowhere, in the middle of the night, in the middle of Pesach!"

"I know all that, Ashi," Tikva answered patiently. "You're right — it would be impossible to *get* a cake. And that's why what we have to do is — to bake it!" Turmoil broke out in the Baker corner, as all the Bakers began talking at once. The old man gave a vehement snore, opened his eyes, refolded his newspaper, glared at the Bakers, and closed his eyes once again. The Bakers quieted down immediately and began speaking in urgent whispers.

"Bake a cake? But how can we possibly bake a cake?"

"And where can we possibly bake a cake?"

"With what could we possibly bake a cake?"

Ashi looked disappointed. He knew his sister Yochie well enough not to have had too much faith in one of her bright "ideas," but when level-headed Tikva had said that she thought that maybe they could do it, his hopes had risen once again. And now, here it was — an idea so ridiculous it was worthy of Yochie herself! Bake a cake!

Rivka put Ashi's thoughts into words. "Tikva, you must be out of your mind! Bake a cake? Sure we could bake a cake — if we had ingredients and an oven to bake it in! All strictly kosher for Pesach, of course," she added sarcastically.

"Look, guys, maybe if you stop arguing about all this, we can get down to details," Yochie said persuasively.

But Rivka was not to be persuaded. "What details? Like where we're going to find the magic wand that'll make a chocolate cake with vanilla frosting magically appear out of nowhere? Or maybe where we can find the phone number of our fairy godmother to ask her if she would take one of Mr. Hot Pepper's dinner napkins and turn it into a strawberry shortcake?"

Yochie giggled. "Actually, if it's Cinderella's fairy godmother, it would probably turn into pumpkin pie! But seriously, you haven't heard the most important part of the plan yet. I think Tikva has guessed it, though."

Tikva spoke up. "I'm not sure if this is exactly what you have in mind, Yochie, but it seems to me that what we have to do is find some family who wouldn't mind having their kitchen invaded in the middle of the night by a bunch of baking Bakers."

Ashi looked interested, hopeful once again.

"You mean bake a cake at somebody's house?"

Tikva nodded. "That's right. We just have to find someone a little unconventional..."

"Who doesn't mind crazy ideas and odd surprises..." added Yochie.

"Who likes to be up late..." Rivka said, practical as always.

"And who has a *kosher l'Pesach* kitchen and all the fixings for a grand birthday cake!" Yochie concluded triumphantly.

The Baker quints looked at each other. Unconventional. A little crazy. Loves surprises. Late night hours. Mixing bowls and measuring spoons and *kosher l'Pesach* potato flour —

"Nechama Orenstein!" they all cried out at once.

"It's just right," said Rivka, enthusiastic at last, thinking about their red-headed friend and classmate at Bais Yaakov of Bloomfield. "She's crazy enough to like the idea. Her family is always up till all hours of the night. They've certainly got a *kosher l'Pesach* kitchen. Perfect!"

"But how will we get there?" asked Dini.

"We can take a cab," Zahava suggested. "But it'll cost money."

"I'd spend a small fortune to be able to get the Shohams that cake!" exclaimed Ashi.

"Then maybe we should bake some fortune cookies," quipped Yochie, exulting in the success of her idea.

For the first time that night since he'd realized his oversight, Ashi smiled broadly.

"No thanks. One nice-sized birthday cake would fit the menu much better!"

The Bakers got up and headed for the phones. They would have to call the Orensteins, and then find a cab. They would have to figure out who was going to go to the great bake-off and who would stay behind. They would have to discuss what kind of cake to bake and how to get it back to the hotel. There was so much to take care of in so little time!

In his armchair, the old man snored gently, fast asleep once again. Ashi Baker looked at him as he rushed out with his sisters. *Sleep well, sir,* Ashi thought cheerfully to himself, knowing that for him, at least, there would be no time to be snoring tonight!

In less time than any of them would have ever thought possible, the Baker kids worked out all the details of the nighttime bake-in. Bracha, always an eloquent spokesperson for the clan, called the Orensteins. Nechama had been on the verge of going to sleep when the phone call came through. She was a bit surprised — well, stunned might describe it better — at the idea of a midnight birthday cake baking party, but with her usual relish for the unusual she agreed to ask her mother if the Baking Bakers could come over. Mrs. Orenstein, by now used to her daughter's escapades, readily consented. Ashi had been concerned about buying the ingredients at such a late hour, and Rivka had wondered where they would find a recipe. Mrs. Orenstein solved all those problems by offering them free use of anything in her kitchen, refusing adamantly Ashi's offer to pay for the supplies they used.

"Just make sure you clean up when you finish — and let Nechama help you lick the bowl!" she told them with a chuckle.

At her house, Nechama, all thought of sleep now forgotten, headed for the Pesach cookbooks to find a recipe that wasn't too hard — but one that was worthy of a Riley Lake Hotel party. She cleaned off the counter, took out all the ingredients from the Pesach cupboard, and readied the mixer and the bowls. Nechama was usually a rather reluctant helper in the kitchen, but not tonight! Not when it came to baking a late-night birthday cake for Avi Shoham himself!

Meanwhile, back at the hotel, Ashi had arranged with the local cab company to come pick up the intrepid baking expedition in fifteen minutes. After some discussion, the Bakers decided that Tikva, the most efficient baker among them, should lead the cake campaign and that Dini, who was good at that sort of thing, should go along to oversee the decorating. Ashi insisted on accompanying the two girls.

"Won't you be too tired to do your job tomorrow morning?" asked a concerned Bracha.

"Do you think I'd sleep a wink until you guys came back with the cake?" Ashi replied somewhat grimly, and that question was settled.

The issue of their parents was a bit trickier. Ashi was adamant in not wanting to ask his parents for help. The girls saw that it was important to their older brother that he succeed as a waiter without his mother and father coming to the rescue, but they were still reluctant to agree to leaving without telling them. They finally convinced Ashi that they should let them know what was going on.

The seven Bakers raced up the stairs to their parents' room. They knocked at the door gently. No answer. They knocked again, a little harder. Ashi held his breath. No answer again.

"Looks like they're asleep already," Ashi finally said, secretly relieved.

"We can't wake them up," said Rivka.

"So what do we do?" asked Yochie, looking crushed. "Do we forget the whole thing?"

Once again, Ashi hardly dared to breathe. What would his sisters decide? Would the plan fall through just now, when they were so close to succeeding?

"No, I don't think so," Tikva answered slowly. "I mean, we can't let Ashi down now. I'm sure that Ima and Abba would agree with that." She gave her brother an encouraging smile. "But there's one thing I'm concerned about. I don't think we should wake them up, but I'm afraid that if they wake up at night and don't find all of us in bed, they'll worry."

"No problem, then," said Yochie, who'd brightened at Tikva's words. "We'll leave them a note in an envelope and tape it to their door." The Bakers raced back downstairs to find writing equipment and hastily penned a note to their parents:

Dear Ima and Abba,

Ashi and Tikva and Dini are okay, they had to run out to get something important done. The rest of us are sleeping soundly. For details, just wake us up.

Love,
The Baking Bakers

The Baker bunch sprinted back up the stairs with their letter, reaching their parents' floor in record time. "It's not exactly the Gettysburg Address, but it'll have to do," said an out-of-breath Yochie, quickly sealing the note and affixing it to Mr. and Mrs. Baker's door.

And then, suddenly, it was time. Ashi grabbed his wallet, his sisters snatched their heavy sweaters, and the three raced back downstairs yet again to await the cab. The rest of the Bakers piled into Yochie's room, which overlooked the front drive of the hotel.

"It's amazing, isn't it? You take one idea, work out a whole bunch of details, and you get a full-blown plan!" said Rivka, who had secretly doubted all along that they would be able to pull it all together so quickly.

"You know, it's sort of like baking a cake," added Zahava. "You take one recipe, work in a whole bunch of ingredients, and you get — a full-blown birthday cake!"

"I certainly hope so," said Bracha tensely.

"What do you mean, Bracha?" asked Zahava.

"Well, I hate to say this, Zahava, but there's one other way that plans are like cakes," answered Bracha, looking earnestly at her sister in the dark room. "There's one other thing that they have in common."

"What's that?" asked her sisters.

"Both can flop," said Bracha nervously. An anxious silence followed.

Yochie had been looking eagerly out the window as the two girls spoke. Suddenly, she spotted them — headlights!

"It must be the taxi," she whispered excitedly.

As the girls watched, three figures detached themselves from the shadows and entered the yellow cab. The taxi turned around, its headlights illuminating the black trees surrounding the hotel for just a moment, and drove away on the dark country road.

12
Having Your Cake...

Just over an hour later, the yellow taxicab, its tires screeching, pulled up into the Orensteins' driveway. The house was dark, except for a faint welcoming light coming from the kitchen. Ashi pulled out his wallet and paid the driver with an inward pang. He'd taken this job to earn some money, and now he was parting with a nice chunk of his savings instead! Still, if he could get Avi Shoham the birthday cake his mother had ordered for him, it would be worth every penny.

Nechama, who'd been watching impatiently from the window for her friends' appearance, ran to open the door, giving them a conspiratorial grin.

"How was the trip?" whispered the spunky redhead. "I can't believe you actually made it!"

"We can't believe it, either," confessed Dini. "Boy, that cabby really was flying!"

"Good thing, too," added Tikva. "We haven't a minute to spare!"

Nechama, who would have loved to remain in the hallway chatting, took the hint and led the Bakers to the kitchen.

"I've set everything up already for you," she said proudly, pointing to the counter where bowls and spoons and all the makings of a chocolate cake were neatly laid out. "I found a recipe that my mother said is pretty foolproof. I even began measuring the sugar and the potato flour."

Dini and Tikva thanked their friend profusely, even as they donned aprons, anxious not to waste any time at all. Dini read the recipe out loud to help her sister, who saw things only dimly by the kitchen light. Working as much by instinct, experience, and feel as by sight, Tikva began separating eggs expertly, mixing Nechama's prepared bowls of sugar and potato flour, adding in the cocoa, folding all the ingredients together to make one unforgettable Pesach birthday cake.

Time went by quickly as the three girls worked together, hardly exchanging a word. Ashi looked on nervously, hoping that it would look good, that it would taste fine, and that they would be back in time for him to set the table for breakfast.

A spoonful of vanilla...a cup of oil...a half cup of strong coffee...there! Tikva finished mixing all the ingredients. She dipped her finger in the batter. It struck her as a bit lumpier than usual, but then it had been a whole year since she'd last made a Pesach cake, and she must have forgotten what the proper consistency should feel like.

Ashi, looking for something to do to help pass the time, had preheated the oven and oiled the pan. Tikva carefully poured the batter and Dini placed the pan in the center of the oven with painstaking care. Forty-five minutes to bake it, then another few minutes to cool and frost — they would be finished in plenty of time!

"What now?" asked Nechama, untying her apron.

"We have to make the frosting and clean up the kitchen," answered Tikva, feeling the tension trickle out of her body.

"But first, we have to follow Mrs. Orenstein's instructions," Dini reminded them, with a grin. "Nechama, you have to lick the bowl!"

Smiling, Nechama ran her finger around the gooey chocolate left in the mixing bowl. She slowly lifted her finger to her mouth, meditatively placed it inside — and immediately began coughing and choking. She raced to the sink for a glass of water, her eyes watering and her face as red as her hair!

"Nechama, Nechama! What is it? What happened?" her friends cried, shocked and alarmed.

Nechama sputtered a little, gave a slight gasp, and was finally able to rasp out a few words.

"I don't know what we put into that cake, but it doesn't taste like any batter I've ever licked!"

Gingerly, Tikva placed her little finger in the bowl and carefully tasted the batter. She made a wry face and quickly took a glass of water.

"Salt," she said shortly. "This batter is chock full of salt..."

"Omigosh!" cried Nechama, running to the cupboard. "I don't believe it! It's all these Pesach packages... they look different from the usual packages. Oh, no, guys, I'm so sorry — I prepared salt instead of sugar!"

Dini groaned. Twenty precious minutes wasted... all those ingredients...and all they had for their pains was a kosher-for-Pesach chocolate cake that Lot's wife might have enjoyed! What would they do now?

Ashi didn't waste any time on what-nows and what-ifs. He was already taking the cake out of the oven, scraping out the salty batter, and cleaning up all the utensils for another try.

"Fast work, Ashi," said Tikva, encouragingly.

"I guess I'm getting used to dealing with disasters this week," her brother answered grimly.

The tension was thicker than whipped egg whites as the three girls resumed their cooking. Dini carefully measured out the sugar — sugar this time! — and the oil and the potato flour. Nechama found another dozen eggs and began cracking them open, checking for blood spots. She actually found one in the fifth egg, and she quickly disposed of it and washed the egg cup.

"I guess that means we need another egg to replace it, plus the eggs for the frosting," she said, and opened the refrigerator to get some more.

A moment later, however, Nechama closed the refrigerator door with a bang and turned to face her friends, her face white.

"But that's the last of the eggs! I can't believe it — we don't have another egg in the house!"

No more eggs! How would they finish the cake? How would they make the frosting? It was past midnight — where would they find eggs in sleeping Bloomfield?

"I don't suppose any store is open this late," said Tikva desperately.

"I don't suppose you have any chickens in your backyard," Dini suggested, almost hysterically.

I don't suppose I'll survive the rest of the week in the children's dining room, Ashi thought bleakly to himself.

"I don't suppose a person can get any sleep around here!" Rabbi Orenstein walked into the kitchen, wearing a maroon bathrobe over his pajamas. "What's all the commotion in here anyway?"

"Oh, Abba," Nechama wailed. "We're all out of eggs!"

"Oh, good," her father answered dryly. "I thought you were simply all out of your minds!"

"But, Abba, we salted the chocolate cake!"

"Oh, is that a new way of cooking up eggs?" her father asked, totally at sea.

"Oh, Abba," Nechama began again, even more incoherently. Finally, Ashi stepped in.

"A *gutten moed*, Rabbi Orenstein," he said, shaking hands with the older man. "We're so sorry to have disturbed you. Your wife said it would be okay for us to bake a cake here tonight, and, well, things have not exactly gone smoothly."

Ashi explained to Rabbi Orenstein how he'd forgotten to order the cake for the Shohams and about their late-night expedition. Mercifully, he glossed over Nechama's little sweet-and-sour mix-up, just saying that the first batch hadn't come out quite right.

Rabbi Orenstein's usually cheerful face looked grave as he listened to Ashi's explanations. He tugged at his red beard thoughtfully.

"Ashi, there's one thing I'm afraid you've forgotten in all this. You can't just go bringing food from the outside into a kosher hotel — and especially not on Pesach! Have you spoken to the *mashgiach* about this cake?" Ashi paled. The *mashgiach*! He hadn't thought about that one at all.

"Oh, no, you're absolutely right! And I can't very well call Rav Landau about it now! Oh, no, there goes the cake! What do we do now?"

Rabbi Orenstein stood motionless for a moment, and then he spoke excitedly.

"Landau? Rav Landau? That wouldn't be Rav Baruch Landau, would it?"

"Yes," answered Ashi glumly, hardly knowing what he was saying. "Yes, I think his first name is Baruch."

"No problem, then! Baruch Landau teaches at the same yeshivah that I do — we have a *Gemara chavrusa* every Wednesday night! I'll just call him first thing tomorrow morning and clear the cake with him."

Color returned to Ashi's pale face. "Oh, Rabbi Orenstein, would you?" he asked eagerly. "I can't believe it! Maybe it'll work out after all!"

"Of course it'll work out," Nechama put in stoutly. "Now that my Abba's here to help, this cake will be baked in no time!"

Rabbi Orenstein looked alarmed.

"I don't know, Nechama. Cake baking is not one of my specialties. And," he added, smiling a little into his red beard, "neither is egg laying. So you still have to solve your original problem."

"Not to worry, Rabbi Orenstein," said Tikva, looking fondly at her brother. "Ashi's solved all his problems tonight so far. I'm sure he'll figure out a way to bake this cake without enough eggs."

Ashi smiled, gratified by his sister's confidence. "Well, the batter is almost ready. I'll just look through some cookbooks and see if any other recipes will work with what we've got."

"Good idea," said Rabbi Orenstein. "Come, we'll all help Ashi."

Silence reigned in the Orenstein kitchen for the next few minutes, punctuated only by the sound of pages turning as the would-be bakers sifted through Mrs. Orenstein's Pesach cookbooks. Finally, Ashi let out a triumphant whoop.

"Here it is! I've found it!"

"What is it? What is it?" they all shouted, Rabbi Orenstein loudest of all.

"Mayonnaise! I was looking through this cookbook and it says here that you can always substitute mayonnaise for eggs! It also has a recipe for egg-free Pesach chocolate frosting!"

"We're on! Grab the mayo, and let's get going!"

Minutes later, the batter was done. Once again, Tikva meticulously poured it into the pan and Dini once more placed it with care into the oven, shutting the door gently.

"Do you think I should lick the batter again?" Nechama asked nervously.

"I guess so," answered Tikva, also tense.

Nechama slowly put her finger into the bowl and covered it with chocolate. She hesitated a moment, closed her eyes — and then — in it went!

An enormous, chocolaty smile split her face.

"Delicious," she said blissfully. "Here, guys, why don't you try some?"

The bowl-licking party only lasted for a few moments. There was still plenty for the baking staff to do! Rabbi Orenstein congratulated all of them and went back upstairs, assuring Ashi once again that he would call his friend the *mashgiach* first thing in the morning. The friends cleaned up the mess from the batter, mixed together the frosting, and sat down for a cup of tea and macaroons while they waited for the cake to finish baking.

"Good night's work, huh, girls?" Ashi asked, smiling gratefully at his sisters and Nechama. "Nothing like a little problem-solving to make the night go by quickly!"

"Can you believe that we took Yochie's half-baked idea..." giggled Dini.

"And baked a whole entire cake out of it!" Tikva finished with a jubilant grin.

"I wish I could solve my own little problem as deliciously," Dini said, remembering with a sigh the difficulties of the children's dining room.

"What's the matter, Dini?" asked Nechama curiously.

Dini described graphically the horrors of the kids' dining room and the fruitless attempts of Idy and herself to control the children there.

"The problem, I think," said Dini, sipping her tea, "is that those kids are so stubborn. It's become a test of wills between us and them. Who can hold out the longest?"

"If they were donkeys," giggled Nechama, "you could do what they do in the old story, either hit them with a stick or dangle a carrot in front of their noses to get them to go where you wanted."

Dini put down her glass so suddenly, some of the tea flew out onto the table. Sopping it up excitedly with her napkin, she exclaimed, "That's it! No more sticks! It's time to try some carrots!"

Ashi had been standing over the oven, peeking in through the glass on the door. "Forget the carrots," he interrupted abruptly, "we've got a birthday cake to finish! I think it's done!"

The three girls raced to the oven. Dini took the cake out and laid it reverently on the table. The smell of chocolate filled the air. The cake stood tall in the middle, flattened just a drop at the sides, looking moist and delicious. They'd done it!

They let the cake cool for a few minutes, and then Dini began the delicate task of decorating. She spread the frosting meticulously and then garnished the cake with *Pesachdik* sprinkles and candies.

"Gorgeous," gushed Nechama. "It looks as good as a bakery cake!"

"Better," said Ashi. "A little artwork and a few candies can do amazing things!"

"They sure can," murmured Dini to herself with an inward smile.

"Well, guys, congratulations," Nechama said as she and Dini wrapped the cake tenderly in silver foil. "A good night's work."

"We couldn't have done it without you, Nechama," Tikva said gratefully.

"Hey, it was nothing. My pleasure," Nechama answered, embarrassed but pleased. She stifled a yawn. "But now, you poor things, you have to shlep all the way back to the mountains." She glanced at the kitchen clock. "Five minutes until the cab is scheduled to come back. Better get moving!"

The Bakers said goodbye hastily and carried their precious burden out to the driveway. The yellow taxi returned, punctual to the moment. Before the taxi had even left silent, sleeping Bloomfield, both Dini and Tikva were fast asleep in the back seat.

But Ashi, holding the cake securely in his lap, was still too wound up to sleep. He thought about all the fiascoes of the week, and of its triumphs, too. He was glad that he had worked his way out of this last disaster. But he realized that, for all his desire to be independent and stand on his own, when it came to a crisis there was nothing like having a family to turn to. Especially a family of Bakers!

The dark sky was beginning to turn pink around the edges and the outline of the brooding mountains just beginning to come clear when the yellow taxi stopped smartly in front of the hotel. Ashi called gently to his sisters to rouse them, and the two girls stumbled sleepily into the hotel, almost sleepwalked into their room, and dropped into bed, not even bothering to change into pajamas. Ashi himself headed straight for his room. Fighting off waves of fatigue, he donned fresh clothing and quickly brought the cake down to the now-open kitchen. A word with the *mashgiach* was enough; Rabbi Orenstein had kept his promise and spoken to his friend just moments before.

The cake safely stowed away, Ashi raced to the shul to daven Shacharis. On his way out, he stopped in the bathroom to splash water on his face and wake himself up for a good morning's work. He looked in the mirror, making sure his bow tie was straight and his collar stiff. Finally, looking just like a Riley Lake waiter should look, Ashi headed into the dining room to set the V.I.P. table for a special birthday breakfast.

13
And Eating It, Too...

Happy birthday, dear Avi, happy birthday to you..."

A breakfast birthday — there was nothing like it! Ashi Baker stood in a corner of the dining room, drinking in the joyous atmosphere of the morning. He remembered cheerfully how Mrs. Shoham had whispered to him as she walked into the room, a step ahead of her son.

"Everything under control?" she'd asked the young waiter in a hushed voice. Happily, he'd been able to give her a quick nod and an almost invisible smile.

The Shohams and Bodners had sat down and ordered their meal. Then the Baker children had rushed in with their usual crash and clamor. Even Tikva and Dini had made it downstairs, though Bracha had to poke them twice to keep them from falling asleep over their melon salad.

Mr. and Mrs. Baker were the last to arrive, carrying Saraleh and Rachel Ahuva with them. After they'd washed on the matzah and said the *brachah*, Mrs. Baker gave her brood a suspicious look.

"There was a very peculiar note stuck to my door this morning," she began. "Anybody here want to explain what it was all about?"

"Hey, Waiter!" Yochie cried, looking at Ashi. "Can we get some breakfast around here?"

Ashi hurried over and began taking seven orders all at once. Mrs. Baker forgot the note, forgot her suspicions, in the chaos of sorting out breakfast.

"We'll have to tell them, you know, some time," Bracha whispered to Yochie.

"Yeah, but let's wait until after the party. We don't want anybody at the next table overhearing!"

Breakfast had gone well. No soup was spilled — no soup was served, so that was an easy one — and no silverware was forgotten. It was almost over when the lights went out suddenly in the large room, and who should walk in, carrying the beautifully decorated, homemade, perfectly *kosher l'Pesach* chocolate birthday cake but — Mr. Heisenpfeffer himself! Ashi walked next to him, carrying two lit sparklers and a colorful bunch of balloons and wearing an enormous smile.

The whole dining room joined in singing "Happy Birthday" to the astonished Avi.

"Speech, speech!" somebody shouted, and all the guests took up the cry.

Avi stood up. The crowd grew silent. The young man cleared his throat and began to speak.

"I'd like to thank my family for arranging such a beautiful surprise for my birthday. Would you believe, I thought they'd forgotten all about it! I'd also like to thank the kitchen staff, especially my waiter, Ashi Baker, for making such a *heimishe simchah* possible in such a beautiful setting.

"I'm not sure what else to say," Avi continued, shy for once in front of an audience. "I guess I've gotten so used to singing *to* people that I've forgotten how nice it is to be sung to! But I really appreciate all your good wishes. *A gutten moed* to you all."

The audience, completely captivated by the charming young man, burst into applause and began spontaneously to sing Avi's trademark song, "*Sheyibaneh Beis HaMikdash.*" What a song! What a breakfast! What a birthday!

"What in the world did that note mean?" Mrs. Baker asked her children again, after the birthday excitement had died down and the family had finished *bentching.*

"Ima, how about coming to sit in our favorite corner of the lobby," suggested Bracha tactfully. "We have a rather amazing story to tell you."

Needless to say, Mr. and Mrs. Baker were astonished at their children's account of the night's excitement. Mrs. Baker was inclined to scold ("Of course you could have woken us up, kids, you can always wake us up in an emergency!") but Mr. Baker was pleased at his children's independence and initiative, and at the way they had worked together as a team.

"You know," he said, "that chocolate cake tasted so good because it had some very special ingredients."

"Like what?" asked Moishy, who'd swallowed his chagrin at having slept through the night's excitement in his admiration for his brother's triumph.

"Like cooperation, like teamwork, and like love," answered Mr. Baker.

"And a whole lot of salt," added the irrepressible Yochie.

"Now Dini and Tikva, I think you both should head straight to your rooms for a nap," said Mrs. Baker. "You had a very late night yesterday!"

"Okay, Ima, I just have to talk something over with Idy for a few minutes, okay?" Dini ran off to talk to her friend.

"Wasn't that a great party?" Idy asked Dini.

"Did you like the cake?" asked Dini innocently.

"Sure! I adore chocolate cake!" her friend answered.

"Well, you're never going to believe who baked it!" exclaimed Dini, telling her amazed friend the details of last night.

"What a fabulous story, Dini," Idy said, when she'd finished.

"But that's not all, Idy! Something Nechama mentioned last night gave me an idea. Here's what I think we should do..."

It took just a few moments for Dini to explain her idea and for the two girls to figure out the details.

"But first," said Idy, "you have to take a nap to give you the energy to make it work...and I have to talk to somebody about something important. Meet you back in the lobby in two hours!"

Dini headed straight up to her room, and Idy headed straight back to the dining room, where her cousin, Avi, was finishing *bentching*.

"Avi, I have to talk to you," she told him earnestly. "You're not going to believe what I have to say..."

A few minutes later, Ashi was hard at work clearing the tables under Mr. Heisenpfeffer's stern eyes. He took a cartload of dirty silverware into the kitchen and then came back to finish gathering the used tablecloth. As he emerged from the kitchen, he was surprised to see Avi Shoham, who'd returned to the dining room from his room, where he had finished packing his bags.

"Hi, Ashi," the young singer told the waiter. "I just wanted to say thank you, and goodbye." Unexpectedly, Avi thrust a sealed envelope into Ashi's hand. "Just a little token of my appreciation."

"Thank you so much," stammered Ashi. He remembered what Mr. Heisenpfeffer had mentioned about tips, but he wasn't prepared for anything — certainly not from Avi Shoham!

"No, no, thank *you*," returned Avi, with a little wink. "You look tired, Ashi," he concluded with a grin. "Maybe you should take a little nap this morning."

"Maybe I should," said Ashi, more and more astonished. "Thanks again."

Avi walked out toward his car, which had been brought around to the front of the hotel. Ashi opened the envelope with shaky fingers. Inside, he found a generous tip, one which would cover his last night's taxi fare, and then some. Even better, he found a handwritten note on Avi Shoham's personal stationery. "To a fine waiter, with appreciation, Sincerely, Avi Shoham," it said, ending with a PS: "Special thanks for a terrific birthday cake. You know what they say: once a Baker, always a baker!"

Dumbfounded, Ashi stared after Avi Shoham's departing car. Then, smiling from ear to ear, he pocketed the note and the money and, humming "*Sheyibaneh Beis HaMikdash*" softly to himself, headed up to his room for a much-needed nap.

14
Dangling the Carrot

Dini woke up an hour later, fresh and rested from her nap. Idy had told her that she was going to go rowing on Riley Lake while Dini slept that morning. Dini ran out to find her friend and to start working on their plan right away.

She met Idy walking with Tikva and Zahava near the hotel dock. The three girls were soaking wet and red in the face. Dini could sense their outrage and their anger. These three hot, wet girls were steaming!

"What happened?" cried an alarmed Dini.

"What happened? Go ask *them* what happened!" Zahava said bitterly.

"Them" were Lenny Blumenberg and Ronnie Pearl, whom Dini could see off on the lake, doubled over with laughter in their rowboat.

"But what happened?" Dini asked again.

"Water balloons," Idy answered shortly.

Apparently, the two boys had gotten hold of the extra balloons from Avi Shoham's party and brought them along for the boat ride. The girls, out for a pleasant trip on the placid waters of Riley Lake, had been their first victims.

"My new dress is ruined!" moaned Zahava. "Those kids are completely out of control!"

"Don't worry, Zahava, it'll dry out fine," Dini comforted her sister.

"But what in the world are we supposed to do about those boys?" Tikva asked.

"Don't worry about that, either," Dini answered confidently. "Idy and I know exactly what we're going to do about them."

"What are you two planning?" questioned Tikva.

"We are planning," her sister answered her firmly, "to feed those boys some carrots." And she and Idy walked off together in the direction of the hotel, her sisters looking after her wonderingly.

"The first thing we have to do, I suppose, is to speak to Mr. Heisenpfeffer," suggested Dini.

"Mr. Hot Pepper! Do we really have to, do you think?"

"Well, it's his dining room, after all, and if we're going to be hanging things up and changing things around..."

"Okay, I guess you're right," Idy said, with a sigh.

"Don't worry, Idy. Remember, he was quite nice the last time we spoke to him, and he seems to like Ashi a little more now."

"True, Dini," answered her friend. "When he came in with Avi's birthday cake, he seemed almost human."

Dini hesitated for a moment, and then plunged in. "To tell you the truth, Idy, I've been feeling a little bad about Mr. Heisenpfeffer. The way we've been talking about him, I mean. We've said a lot of *lashon hara* about him, I'm afraid. And it certainly isn't nice of us to call an old man Hot Pepper!"

Idy looked contrite. "I never thought about it that way," she said slowly. "What do you think we should do now?"

"Well, I've been thinking about it. It's not like we can go over and tell him, Mr. Heisenpfeffer, sir, we've all been talking about how crabby and grumpy you are and calling you names, can you forgive us? That'll only make him feel bad!"

"I guess that's one of the worst things about *lashon hara*," said Idy wisely. "It's so hard to make up for it."

"I suppose the best thing we can do is to be more careful from now on. No more hot pepper jokes!"

The two girls walked together, thinking seriously about the head waiter and how they would be more careful about their speech in the future. They found Mr. Heisenpfeffer in the dining room, as usual, barking orders at the waiters, who were setting up for lunch.

"Excuse us, Mr. Heisenpfeffer, could we ask you something?" Dini asked, a little timidly.

"You're the two girls who are trying to fix things up in the children's dining room, aren't you?" the head waiter asked gruffly. "How has it been going so far?"

"Not too well, I'm afraid, Mr. Heisenpfeffer. That's what we want to talk to you about."

"Come to my office, right in the corner of the kitchen, and we'll discuss it," the old man said.

Idy and Dini hadn't even noticed the tiny cubicle where the head waiter had his desk. The wall was covered with pictures of the hotel. Dini noticed with wonder the carefully marked file folders holding menus of years past, ideas for future meals, details about the hotel staff, and the like.

"Now what exactly would you young ladies like to do about the ruckus in the children's dining room?"

Dini, the spokesperson, explained what she and Idy had in mind. As she talked, it seemed to her that the lines on the head waiter's craggy face softened, his mustache grew less alarmingly stiff, his expression turned less threatening.

Dini finished talking and sat silently, not sure of what would come next. Mr. Heisenpfeffer cleared his throat, and then said, unexpectedly, "You girls think I'm a crotchety old man, don't you?"

"No, no, of course not," Dini answered, stumbling over her words in her confusion.

Mr. Heisenpfeffer continued thoughtfully. "I guess I can seem sort of mean, especially to youngsters like you. I know I have a bad temper — always have had one. Would you believe that when I was young my friends used to call me Hot Pepper?"

Idy blushed deep red. Dini sat staring, uncertain of whether to answer or not.

"Well, young ladies, if I seem very tough sometimes, it's because I love this hotel. There aren't many things that are run right in the world nowadays. People aren't careful about things, don't try to make them perfect. Cars break down, machines fall apart, nothing is built to last." Mr. Heisenpfeffer spoke almost to himself, as if he'd forgotten that the two girls were there.

"I haven't too much to care about in this world, but I do care about the Riley Lake Resort Hotel. Whatever I do, I want to do it right. If my job is to make guests happy here, to run a clean and efficient kitchen and a happy dining room, I want to do that right, too."

"And you are, Mr. Heisenpfeffer, you are," said Dini without thinking.

"Oh, do you think so? I'm glad." A fleeting smile flashed at the two girls and then disappeared behind the iron gray mustache.

"I don't know what's got into me today, talking to you like this, and right before lunchtime, too," continued Mr. Heisenpfeffer. "Guess I'm getting old. But what I want you to know is, I'm glad to see young people caring about setting things right. Not many do nowadays, you know. The only thing I've never been able to get working right is that children's dining room. So anything you want to do to fix it up — go right ahead!"

The two girls felt both exhausted and exhilarated as they left the office.

"Did what I think just happened really happen?" Idy asked her friend, wide-eyed.

"It sure did!" exclaimed Dini.

"I feel worse than ever about calling him Hot Pepper," Idy said sadly.

"You know, I think the best thing we can do now is to get that dining room working right, as he would say, to try to make up for it. So let's get going and start on the plan!"

The two girls raced off to a small cottage behind the main hotel building where arts and crafts supplies were kept. They explained to the arts counselor exactly what they wanted to do and got to work. Only an hour until lunchtime — they had to work fast if they were to be on time!

With only minutes to spare, the two girls raced down with their art project, back to the kitchen. Hastily, they outlined to the chef what they would need. The chef asked Mr. Heisenpfeffer for his permission, and the head waiter answered shortly that he was to give the two girls whatever they asked for.

Next, the girls walked over to Yudy Friedman, who was disconsolately setting the tables in the children's dining room. "Only one day more, only one day more," he kept murmuring to himself. He wondered why he bothered setting the tables nicely at all, knowing that within minutes the place would look like a garbage dump on a bad day.

The two girls interrupted Yudy's dark musings with their request to set things up in the dining room.

"We think we've really got something that'll make things here run smoothly," Dini explained eagerly.

Yudy looked doubtful, but he agreed to help arrange things and to keep the dining room doors closed until the girls were ready.

Grabbing a stepladder, Dini climbed and hung up the project.

"Not a bad-looking 'carrot,' is it, Idy?" she asked with some pride.

Twelve o'clock. High noon at the Riley Lake Resort Hotel. The children who ate in the kids' dining room were lining up outside. Lenny Blumenberg rattled at the doors.

"Hey, it's lunchtime already! Let us in! We're starving!"

One more bag to nail on. Put the stepladder away. Plug in the lights. Get ready, get set....

Yudy Friedman threw open the doors to the children's dining room. Fifty loud, hungry, rambunctious youngsters stormed in, ready to begin pushing and shouting and fighting as usual.

Lenny and Ronnie, at the head of the mob as always, stopped suddenly in their tracks, causing six children behind them to bang into each other with a thud and a boom.

"Hey, guys, what's that?"

"That" was a huge poster, drawn on colored posterboard in cheerful colors. "Welcome to the Riley Lake Kids' Dining Room," it said on top. Underneath, the name of every child who ate in the room was drawn in fancy lettering. Flashing colored lights edged the whole production, lending it an especially festive air.

But, most remarkable of all, underneath each child's name was a small plastic bag full of *Pesachdik* candies.

"Wow," said Miri Freedberg, staring up at the unexpected sight. "That's awesome!"

Idy and Dini let the crowd look at the poster, wonder about it and admire it for a few moments. Then, standing up on chairs in front of their creation, they held up their hands for attention.

"Ladies and gentlemen," Dini began, speaking softly so the children would have to be quiet to hear her, "what you see in front of you is the official Riley Lake Poster Reward Game."

"The what?" a chorus of voices cried out.

"It works like this. At every meal Idy and I will fill a bag with treats — candies, lollipops, fruits, cookies. Anybody who behaves at that meal will be entitled to take their bag back to their room. Anybody who doesn't," she added bluntly, "won't."

"And to make it even more interesting," Idy continued, "in each bag there is a Good Kid coupon. Save it, because at the end of Pesach whoever has ten or more of these will be entitled to a prize, donated by Mr. Heisenpfeffer himself!"

Would it work? Dini held her breath. They had tried shouting and cajoling and threatening — all of the sticks that they could think of. Now, here it was — not a carrot, exactly, but something the children liked, dangling right in front of their eyes, where it would remind them that there was more to hotel life than food fights and water balloons. Would it work?

It did! That day's lunch was a meal that Idy, Dini, and especially Yudy Friedman would never forget. The room was noisy, but it was controlled noise. Once, Lenny Blumenberg forgot himself and began throwing an apple at Ronnie Pearl.

"The candies, Lenny, the candies," Ronnie hissed at his friend, and the two sat down quietly once again.

Food stayed on the plate or was put politely in the mouth; silverware stayed on the napkin or in the hand; soda remained unmixed with four different types of juice. By the time it was all over, Yudy Friedman felt confident enough to believe that maybe it would be safe one day to bring another bottle of seltzer into the room!

As lunch ended, Idy and Dini distributed the bags with a smile. They knew that there might be occasional setbacks. One day no doubt Ronnie or Lenny or one of the other lively children would forget and give in to the urge to shout or push or shpritz. On that day, though, that child and any others involved in the brouhaha wouldn't get a bag — and that might be enough to stop him or her the next time.

What's more, Dini and Idy believed that when the children themselves saw how much more pleasant the meal was with talking instead of shouting, joking instead of throwing, they would come to behave a little better for their own sakes, and not just for the candy.

Lunchtime over, the two kid-tamers ran out of the dining room, congratulating themselves. They'd done it! They were sure that the rest of the *chag* would proceed smoothly after this. Their first stop was back to the kitchen, to get more plastic bags and to plan with the chef for the next set of treats.

On their way out of the kitchen, Idy and Dini met Mr. Baker, walking quickly to the *beis medrash*, where the *rav* was about to begin an afternoon *shiur*.

"Where are you two going off to in such a hurry?" he asked the girls amiably.

"Oh, just off to plant some more carrots," they answered him happily. Mr. Baker gave the girls a puzzled smile as they ran off in the direction of the art room and a whole new set of Good Kid coupons for the good kids of the children's dining room.

15
Bracha's Diary #2

Dear Diary,

Well, here we are back home in good old Bloomfield. Hard to believe it, after the exciting week we had at Riley Lake. Sorry about not filling you in on the details as they happened there. It's been ages since I had time to even think about writing. First there were those hectic Pesach cleaning days, and then came Pesach itself. You might not know it, Diary, but you're not supposed to write on Chol HaMoed if at all possible, so I haven't been able to tell you all the happenings at the hotel.

And what happenings they were! Riley Lake, Smiley Lake — absolutely, positively no mistake! Our days and nights at the hotel were hopping with things to do and see over Chol HaMoed. There were sports galore — I was the star of the girl's basketball game one morning — and swimming every day. We went on nature walks and hikes all over the area. What a beautiful way to wel-

come the springtime! It was drizzly one day so we spent the morning playing Ping-Pong and listening to our new Avi Shoham CD over and over and over again. In the afternoon, we all jumped into the car and went roller skating in Mountainville, a sweet little town nearby.

Just to keep things interesting, every night there was something else to do, too. Zahava especially loved the fashion show, and we all enjoyed circus night, with its clowns and magicians. Spectacular!

But as much as I had fun with all the running around, I think I liked the quieter days of Yom Tov even better. Ima gave more shiurim to the hotel girls, by popular demand, and we enjoyed walking around the grounds and just talking. I made friends with another girl, Chanie Goldberg, from New York City. We got pretty close in the last few days, and we've promised bli neder to try to write to each other. Hope we keep it up.

The real heroes of the week, though, were Ashi and Dini and Idy. Ashi finished his first real job on a high note. I mean that literally — on the last day of Yom Tov he sang a duet at the table with Avi Shoham, who came back at the end of Chol HaMoed. Mr. Heisenpfeffer was really pleased with our Ashi, and told him that he could be sure of a job in the hotel any time bein hazmanim.

Incidentally, Dini gave us a real mussar shmooze about Mr. Heisenpfeffer. She made us realize that we'd acted pretty rotten, making fun of him. (She didn't use the word rotten so we wouldn't feel so bad, but I can be honest with you, Diary.) I think we've all learned a lesson from what happened. It made it even worse that we all realized that underneath his rather abrupt manner is a nice, caring man. I almost cried when he came over on our last morning at the hotel to give us all a personal goodbye.

And I think that Dini did cry, a little at least, when he gave her and Idy their special goodbye gift — a beautiful Certificate of Appreciation from the hotel management for all their help. Diary, you simply would not believe what those two did for the children's dining room! They earned the gratitude of the hotel, of the waiters, and even of the kids themselves. Ronnie Pearl and Lenny Blumenberg actually gave them a gift from all the children. Dini and Idy left the hotel bearing a beautiful poster that all the kids made that said, in big, bright red lettering, "We Love You, Dini and Idy!"

So it was a gorgeous, glorious, indescribable week for the Baker clan this Pesach at the Riley Lake Hotel. No wonder, then, that we were all a little gloomy as we piled into the car to go home the day after Pesach.

We were on the road for just a few minutes when Abba honked the horn twice.

"It's too quiet in here," he announced. "I can't keep my mind on the driving if there's no noise."

"Let's play a game," suggested Ima.

"Geography!" shouted Moishy and Chezky at the same time.

Abba grinned. "Noise level going up already. Good work, gang!"

"Let's start with Israel again," Ima suggested.

"Los Angeles," Dini contributed.

"San Francisco," Zahava continued.

"Oklahoma," Chezky added.

"No A's," I found myself reminding them. "You know the Baker rule: No A's!"

"How about if there's an A that doesn't end in another A?" Chezky asked, a little defensively.

"Like what? Name one!" challenged Yochie.

Chezky thought hard. Then harder. Nothing came.

Dini leaned over toward him and whispered something.

"Antwerp!" Chezky shouted triumphantly.

Yochie, not wanting to be outdone, said she was going to come up with the next one.

"And it's going to be a goodie," she warned, holding her head in concentration.

"Poland?" suggested Moishy.

"Nah," said Yochie, "Too boring. We always say Poland."

"How about Poughkeepsie?"

"Nope," Yochie answered promptly. "Too hard to spell."

"Panama?"

"No," Yochie replied. "Too wet."

"Yochie, that's ridiculous," I said.

"But she can't use it anyway. That's another A word," Rivka objected.

"I got it!" shouted Moishy. "Punjab!"

"Punjab? Did he say Punjab?" Chezky asked.

"I like it!" exclaimed Yochie. "It's unusual, it's exotic — Punjab...Punjab it is!"

"*Glad you approve of it, Yochie,*" *Moishy said dryly.* "*Bet you don't even know where it is.*"

"*Sure I do,*" *answered Yochie.* "*It's in...it's near...it's at...*"

"*No such place!*" *Chezky shouted.*

"*Is too...*"

"*Is not...*"

"*Is too...*"

"*Is not...*"

Abba honked the horn again, with a big smile on his face.

"*Now as far as the noise goes, we're doing fine! We're also doing okay as far as Geography goes. Sorry, Chezky, there is such a place as Punjab. It's in India or Pakistan, I forget which.*"

"*That leaves us with the letter B,*" *Tikva pointed out.*

Yochie turned to Ashi.

"*Hey, Waiter, what can you come up with for B?*" *she asked him.*

"*B? Only one place that matters that starts with B,*" *Ashi answered with a smile.*

"*Bloomfield!*" *we all shouted at once.*

Coming Up Next In
BAKER'S DOZEN

The Baker kids have discovered a secret; they believe their father is going bankrupt! The kids all brainstorm ways to earn money. They're doing it to save the family, but pretty soon it becomes a competition between the boys and the girls. Who can make the most money? The boys do chores for the neighbors and the girls open a health spa in their basement. All goes well with the spa, as long as their parents don't know about it…

Meanwhile, Tikva is facing her own personal challenge. As her class learns about astronomy and goes stargazing, Tikva feels left out. How can she be a part of the class's exciting project when she can't even see the stars?

Join the Baker family as they learn lessons and face surprises in Baker's Dozen #9: *Through Thick and Thin*.